What I Did
For Love

What I Did
For Love

Tessa Dane

Winchester, UK
Washington, USA

First published by Bedroom Books, 2015
Bedroom Books is an imprint of John Hunt Publishing Ltd., Laurel House, Station Approach,
Alresford, Hants, SO24 9JH, UK
office1@jhpbooks.net
www.johnhuntpublishing.com
www.bedroom-books.com

For distributor details and how to order please visit the 'Ordering' section on our website.

Text copyright: Tessa Dane 2014

ISBN: 978 1 78535 034 4
Library of Congress Control Number: 2015930441

A CIP catalogue record for this book is available from the British Library.

Design: Stuart Davies

Printed in the USA by Edwards Brothers Malloy

We operate a distinctive and ethical publishing philosophy in all
areas of our business, from our global network of authors to
production and worldwide distribution.

For the wonder and blessings of my brothers in my life.

I

I am lying on a narrow bed, a soft white robe tied loosely at my waist. The room is shadowed; there is another bed, a deep sofa, wooden furniture, a large, strange curved shape like a saddle covered in velvet sitting on the floor. The door opens and he comes in quickly, silently, pulling his own robe open, and he drops to the great pillow cushions on the floor at the side of my bed. With a flick of his hand, my robe is half open, my left breast exposed, the nipple hard. He caresses it, and then bends and takes my breast in his mouth, giving me little bites and tongue-flicks. I am hot for this man, his effect on my body a drowning of the senses, pleasure, and the nip followed by the kiss and passage of his lips over and over along my breast. "I am going to leave your breasts very sore," he murmurs, a cool voice thick with desire. I do not care.

He said he would use me. This man, who just days ago I thought I could love and desire forever, now hated me and had bought my body in exchange for money, though not in the usual way these things are done. I was not an escort or prostitute – though I may now qualify for these names. He wanted to punish me for rejecting him, and did not know what pain that rejection had cost me, the greater pain I would have had if I had not rejected him.

All these thoughts were flashes of color in a muddle of sexual arousal, his hands moving over my belly, and downward, exploring and finding my quick, working me and then stopping, so that I was ready to faint into unconsciousness of anything but lust, desire, and the pounding of my heart that I could feel tremoring my whole body.

"I am not going to care for your pleasure," he had said coldly and with a cruel smile. "I intend to have every pleasure from you, though. I've never been with a whore, so you're my first." The words were intended as blows, but my moral sense was off somewhere else. By giving myself to this man, I could rescue my brother, his investments, his financial career, and most importantly, I could assure his emotional survival. *My brother would not take my money. I was rich enough, but he was determined to protect my fortune, even if it meant the loss of his own.*

So I lay here with the man who had purchased me, crazed with arousal. I heard him mutter, "I can't wait, even though I wanted to do all sorts of things to you." He rose abruptly from the pillows, pushing aside the rest of my robe, and bending swiftly to suck and give darting licks to the firebox between my legs. "Spread them wide apart," he ordered, his open hands pushing my legs outward from the inside of my thighs. He came over me, his erection quickly glimpsed, and he was pressing into me, I gasping a little, wet enough, the chemistry of us powerful, and his quick thrusts, four or five or six, then stopping and rearranging me, scooping my buttocks, grabbing my hips and moving me upward on the bed, then entering me again.

"I want this to last a long time," he said in a stern whisper. "I want you to be sore everywhere when this night is over."

As if I cared. But it was so strange how all this had happened, that what had started as such sweet love, had come to this.

II

I never had an argument with my brother until that fated day that I also met Grenville Rand. That day our three lives became entangled in love and hate, in ways no one could have predicted. My name is Dray Cooper. Bredon is my older brother and, until this past spring, my legal guardian. He continues to be my self-appointed surrogate father, indulgent, loving, giving me almost everything I want. But our hearts are burdened by sadness, for what he and I want most, only heaven can give. Our parents had been killed three years before on a flight from Paris to New York, their plane exploding from a terrorist's bomb. I was fifteen when they perished, and Bredon was thirty-five. He had been their "honeymoon baby," and I was their "change of life surprise."

Our parents' estate, bequeathed equally to us, left us very rich. Airline settlements and insurance policies added several more millions to each of our fortunes. Bredon's goal was to give me a life that I was not even sure I wanted any more after our parents' violent end. He hired therapists for me, but he was the best help, serving as the anchor for my heart in our now-shaken world. While doctors dealt with my body and psyche under my brother's watchful eye, he was also shaping my financial security. His goal was to protect my inheritance, maximize my income, limit my risk as much as possible. He was a successful financier involved in many high-risk investments, but only let me invest with him if it was "done before begun," if the profit was practically jumping to rapid heights as the venture started. That was a rare thing. Mostly, my money remained in extremely conservative accounts and investments. When I turned eighteen during this, my first college year, my money became my own. My parents had not doubted my ability to handle the wealth they left me, nor Bredon's ability to invest it wisely for me. Bredon had most of my assets hidden behind bland, untraceable corporate names and made sure that all taxes on all my profits were promptly paid. He was not one of the many fools who thought they could evade the IRS forever. He had established two additional trusts that would come to me at twenty-one, "just in case," he had teased me. Just in case I went wild with spending. I never did. My interests were art, science, nerdy things, organizations that protected animals and the environment.

While he guarded the safety of my money, risks were the stuff of Bredon's wealth. It had made him rich in his own right, as a venture capitalist. After his Ivy League college days, with startup money from our parents, Bredon launched an investment group whose bold financial moves and successes had impressed even the so-called Wall Street wizards. High-powered, energetic, his special talent lay in creating profitable new companies. He was unafraid to do testing and product offerings that often seemed too risky and over-the-top to other investors. In the face of skeptics, he would create companies that in turn created new "needs," and dominated brand new markets. Our parents had been surprised, happy, proud that he used his own trust funds and their gifts to continue the tradition of wealth in our family.

I was not ignorant of the ways in which my family had become rich a couple of generations ago, and how it had remained that way. In our private dinner discussions, our parents told us stories of their businesses and investments, and their own parents' and grandparents' financial coups. None of this went beyond the family. We had learned early that no family business or financial planning was ever to be discussed in public.

Bredon's ongoing tutelage gave me a deep understanding of the modern financial world. And after our parents' deaths he also made sure I knew all the details of his investments and projects. I had full access to his accounts, and he would update me on all their passwords. The world saw me as a young girl, which indeed I was, but age disappeared into necessity and my youth hardly mattered. I was smart, and if I could learn the advanced sciences of my high school classes, I could learn the art and science of making and keeping money. After all, men had entered Yale at fourteen years old in the early days of our country. The very young have more possibilities than people believe today. They are legal adults at eighteen, but are often still treated as dependent children. It makes them feel helpless, prolonging their dependency, expecting their parents to solve every problem.

My parents had no patience for that. They expected understanding, and got it. They praised resourcefulness and problem solving, and we responded to that praise. They had also impressed upon us the importance of family in investing and holding our wealth, and using our skills to maintain our fortunes. My brother and I were the family that mattered now, for although we had cousins and great-aunts, we were all that directly remained of our parents.

Privacy was an over-arching concern of my family, as it typically was of the long-time wealthy rich. But privacy is difficult in a media-driven world. It was public knowledge, for instance, that Bredon was our parents' executor and my legal guardian. In the days after the bombing, the media was wild with rumors, reports, commentary, official statements from several governments; the reporters kept stirring up interest with new angles on the story. They sought every detail online and by gossip, about the famous passengers who had died, and the identities of their rich and newly-rich heirs. Our parents were the only American notables on that flight, but several other well-known society "names" from Europe had been on board. Their families too were hounded by their countries' news media.

Most of our friends sympathized as we avoided reporters and hid from them when necessary. We would look straight ahead, ignoring questions asked or shouted at us when we appeared on the street. Endless newspaper articles, television shows and digital news feeds, discussed the tragedy. Public and commercial radio and television aired programs with panel after panel, on terrorism, flying safety, legal issues, possible military retaliation. Bredon and I avoided reading, looking, listening. We did not attend nor watch the press conferences held by government officials about the bombing, where they tried to explain why our parents' plane had been targeted. It was a commercial flight, middle-class families and poorer families also on board, their loved ones suffering and grieving as much as we were.

The evidence was scanty, and pointed to the relentless malice and spite of a small cult of religious extremists, evil men of bitter ignorance, using guns and bombs to defend Almighty God. The blasphemy of such presumption could not penetrate their distorted mental processes. Were it not such a travesty of religious ardor, it would have been the ultimate cosmic joke. All the media talk was really an attempt to deal with fear, to gain reassurance that we were not going to experience another September eleventh. The pictures of various terrorists that appeared in all the visual media made me want to be sick, to empty my body and mind of the images of such murderous, treacherous psychopaths.

Bredon's friends were very careful to respect our privacy and stoic grief. They avoided asking or saying anything indelicate, except for one, who made an appalling blunder. Head of his own investment group, maybe envious of us as two rich siblings, completely ignoring the gut-deep hurt we still carried, this supposed friend made a too-hearty, sarcastic joke that infuriated my brother. A greedy smirk on his face, he told Bredon that even an heiress's brother was entitled to legal fees as the administrator of her estate. Bredon went cold, dead silent.

The jokester was too stupid to see the startled looks of warning and retreat on the faces around them, the palpable silence. In other times a tasteless comment might simply have been ignored or shrugged off, but this one had unleashed my brother's anger, quiet and lethal. Bredon became distant, dismissive when the man was around, disappearing from his life, no calls returned, no requested meetings agreed to. Even as the truth dawned, he did not really understand his blunder. Everyone in their circle was mystified at his tedious stupidity. At last, prompted by exasperated friends, he offered reluctant apologies, which Bredon civilly accepted. Still, the friendship was finished. As word spread that Bredon wanted nothing to do with someone so crass, investors also backed away from the man, because he was now perceived as having shaky judgment.

Again with their friends' intervention, Bredon relented somewhat, and endorsed an investment offering the fellow was making. Though it helped, his full range of clients and the power had yet to be regained. I was relieved that Bredon had shown mercy, and told him so. But the incident was clear warning to stay away from "advising" Bredon on anything concerning me. It was a social firewall, like the one he had set on his businesses so that none of his venture liabilities could ever touch me.

Following our parents' long-ago instructions (it seemed so very long ago), Bredon and I never publicly said anything about each other. I lived my New York life, attending college, sharing my love of the city and its culture with my friends and my brother and his inner circle. Those in my own circles had learned, from my angry eyes and cold exit, not to question me about my brother or my family. The women at my college knew Bredon to be a socialite, a "catch," unmarried. They did not know that my brother's heart was spoken for, that his marriage announcement would have been made on the day after our parents' return. Hardly anyone knew, for he and his fiancée had kept clear of gossip columnists and social reporters. At least a few of the more eager social climbers at my college had looked for an introduction to Bredon, frustrated at my unresponsiveness to their overtures and invitations. Only my closest friends had met my brother before the bombing, and now only Robin had met him beyond a quick introduction.

When Bredon and I spent time together and had the strength for it, we would talk about our parents, recounting familiar stories, laughing, tearful. Bredon had told me more than once that our parents had always asked him to look after me if anything happened to them. "Take care of your sister." They only said it a hundred times, maybe, Bredon kidded me, warming me. Only when we were totally alone would we openly cry with each other. The nights when I had screamed myself awake from my nightmares finally seemed to be over. I think they also died, of exhaustion. I do not know if Bredon had such nights. His focus was on getting me through it. He had doctors on call for me as I went through the daily motions mechanically, my heart feeling dead within me. I had slowly come back to life, but of course it was a different life for both of us now.

I still had occasional nightmares over our parents' deaths, and though I tried to hide them from Bredon, I did slip once. I had a private dorm suite at my college in upper Manhattan, so that my brother's early morning calls wakened only me. That morning my guard was down. I was sleepy, having been up late studying for mid-terms, then had fallen asleep to dreams so horrific, they had left me shaken. I must have sounded wild in my sorrow as Bredon asked his usual "How are you, how is everything?" As he pressed me, I told him I had dreamt of our parents' death. Saying it aloud led me to break down, unable to control the tears that sobbed through as I spoke.

My brother waited for a pause, then said very calmly, "Get dressed and wait for me in front of the college gates." He had hung up before I could protest. I scrambled into my clothes, running to Broadway, few people on the streets at that hour. Bredon had canceled his appointments, ordered his private car, and picked me up within twenty minutes of our call.

After a strong hug, all in silence, we drove up the Henry Hudson Parkway to Fort Tryon Park. We spent the morning in the privacy of trees and back trails, walking, talking, with tears, with remembrances, with another hug now and then. Composed at last, we visited the park's jewel, The Cloisters, to contemplate the incredible sculptures and paintings and tapestries born of faith and hope, and to pity the poor hunted unicorns. Thus did we cope. On special days, their birthdays, their wedding anniversary, and the overwhelming anniversary of their deaths, we visited the Columbarium where our parents' names were inscribed as memorials, though even their ashes had been lost at sea.

Life went on, as it always does. Bredon had arranged the purchase of my apartment in one of buildings his corporation owned, which was just being renovated and reoccupied. Pretending he was looking for a hideaway or extra investment, asking for my opinion, I fell in love with the place that now was mine. It was in a charming old building that extended back onto a quiet side street. The small corner apartment gathered light through its wonderful great windows. Bredon had wanted me to take one of the larger apartments, but this one-bedroom place was my true nest. Over the school year, I would take some time to choose among the treasured pieces from our parents' and grandparents' loved antiques, but I kept the furnishings to a minimum, preferring air and light.

Bredon commissioned the shaping of the apartment to suit me. There was a curving niche off my bedroom that extended along one wall facing the park, which would be my study area. A full bath was next to my bedroom, a little powder room near the front door for guests. A hall led from my bedroom to the long living room where one side, near the small kitchen, served as a dining area. On the other side was a baby grand piano, one of the smallest models. After two years had passed I could finally play music again, though it was a halting return to something I had greatly loved.

When I asked for the small piano, my brother proposed that

he convert two adjoining apartments into one, to have room for an enormous Steinway B, a concert grand that would match the one in his penthouse. I declined, telling him that I would use his piano if I wanted to play some great thundering piece with full keyboard echoing in a large space.

"I'm still waiting," he would say occasionally, although I had in fact used his piano several times when he was traveling. When he was home I preferred listening to him, gifted jazz man that he was. I favored the classics, but Bredon would improvise a jazz line woven around lines from Chopin, just as my teacher used to do. My piano teacher had also taught my brother many years before, and he was an old man when I took lessons from him. His Juilliard training shone through in his command of theory and his beautiful ways of explaining it. I loved learning the many devices a skilled pianist could use, as well as the classical and text-perfect ways of playing the music on the page. But I learned a few standard songs just to hear our parents sing. They had loved music and had sweet, graceful voices. When they sang together it was like love in musical form. They always held hands and sat so close together, each pressed against the other. It was so beautiful, it would leave me in wonder. Such love. Amazing to behold.

Bredon sent me to the Steinway store to pick a piano that suited, and I also had to get some things for the apartment on my own. I haunted the antiques galleries, alone and with my friend Robin, to find the exactly perfect desk that now sat in the niche facing the gorgeous park view. The arc of the desk matched the curve of the wall, its ancient cherry patina and clever drawers inviting to the student and the writer. A comfortable chair, low bookshelves at either end of the niche, cushions for the window seats, and I had my perfect little study. Its open arched doorway adjoined my bedroom which held a queen-size bed for my restless sleep. A huge closet built into one wall held the drawers and shelves that made extra furniture unnecessary.

There was another advantage in the elegant old buildings Bredon had selected for the search: the apartments had back entrances. Years ago, and sometimes even now, these were service entrances leading to freight elevators, back stairways, incinerators, places to store mops and pails. These back doors dated from the old days of live-in servants, when only they would deal with cleaning, laundry, and trash. But those back doors served also as an escape route that Bredon wanted me to have. He had paid for the same advantages in his building. Our parents' death and the publicity aftermath had left us feral, like wild creatures who make sure that their lairs always have a way out if an intruder managed to get inside. We were known, yet we avoided being photographed when at all possible. Even the gentler editors from some of the magazine and websites, who requested interviews with great delicacy and tact, were sweetly thanked by Bredon's assistant, who firmly closed the conversation with, "Perhaps at some future date. We will let you know." That future date, as far as we were concerned, would be never.

Right after the semester ended I moved permanently from my dorm suite and the guest bedroom in Bredon's apartment, to what was now my own home. Bredon had offered me the choice to remain with him, but I wanted the quiet and solace of a space where I could re-make my place in the world. He gave me his reluctant, loving, sad agreement, and my move was done. We were anyway both uptown, near enough to reach each other quickly.

Wealth made it all so possible. My brother did love being rich, and of course the temptation was always there to grow even richer if opportunity permitted. This was the New York financial scene, beautiful offices in gleaming mirrored buildings, elegant facades covering the clawing and scheming over money and its global reach. Money was the center of it all, and the dreadful reason for those first tense words with my brother. On that day, as so often happens, one step, one decision, one "yes" or one "no," and the rest of one's life is never the same.

III

That Monday I had to go to Bredon's office at two o'clock to sign a tax form. He had told me that his receptionist and guard-dog assistant, Mrs. Andrews (we never called her by her first name), would be out that day, so the reception area was empty as I arrived. Bredon and I were high profile in this building, so I had known to dress in chic Manhattan fashion. Forgoing my college "uniform" of jeans and sweatshirts, I wore a fashionably swaying skirt and layered top, a very-latest type of light jacket over my arm, a relatively small handbag, exclusive and chic. I hated handbags and loved pockets, to the dismay of "fashionistas," and never got the point of the handbag obsession. I kept clutching the strap lest I forget it.

All these expensive clothes were gifts from Bredon, thanks to a Bergdorf personal shopper and a designer whose style he liked. But I refused to wear the outrageous five inch high heels that were in fashion. They looked like torture. Why not bind our feet like in old China, and have women hobbling about until their revolution freed them? Despite the protests that many women walked in them easily, and Bredon's offer to have the shoes handmade so that they would be comfortable, I settled on a moderate heel and sheer hose. My long hair, a kind of gold brown with subtle blonde streaks, was the work of an inspired woman in a quiet east side salon. I had pulled it into a velvet tie at the nape of my neck, not swinging glamorously, but obviously a "coiffure," and not a basic hairstyle. I did not look like an office worker, nor like a college girl, but like a young woman whose time was her own. I had sprayed and dabbed on perfumes, and misted some cologne on my clothes. It produced a sensation of roses. I could catch the fragrance only occasionally because the sense of smell tires so easily. My brother, though, would grin with approval. His tiny, gentlemanly sniff of appreciation delighted me.

Rose perfume was special. "Mother would have loved this scent on you," Bredon once – only once – told me. The fragrance brought back the incomparable perfume of the roses we had loved in India, where we had traveled as a family for my thirteenth birthday. Thus today, as on so many other days, the dress and scent were for Bredon, to reassure him that I was all right, that I had survived the tragedy that had stunned us into catatonic disbelief when we had first heard the news.

I was about to walk straight into his office but heard male voices. Bredon and another man were just coming out. Each of them possessed a strong presence like an aura, but I felt a jolt as I looked at Bredon's visitor. I was used to the power that my brother seemed to exude, the excitement women told me they felt when they saw him. Because I was impervious to his attractiveness, I used to be amused that his effect was so compelling. Obviously my parents had instilled the incest taboo quite strongly in us. Added to that was our age difference and, with our parents' urging, Bredon's parental sense of responsibility for my safety and my fate. Other women saw that too, not only at my college. At parties and gatherings many a woman had tried to become friends with me in the hope that Bredon would pay more attention to her as a result of her connection to me.

So I knew about attraction and power, but now I felt it for myself, that air-shimmering effect this man was having on me, that I had seen in other women's reaction to Bredon. The sensation startled me. I wondered if I looked as amazed as I felt as his magnetism pulled me. It was like a romance novel or a fairy tale, the bolt out of the blue, desire, love, lust, whatever. He caught me with his virility, his presence producing a tiny shock of electrical current that touched me everywhere.

He had the well-tailored look of the super financier he undoubtedly was, slender enough, some substance to him. He looked assured and powerful, but best of all he was handsome without being pretty, his dark blond hair perfect for his regular, serious features. I was startled by his effect on me because I had never before just looked at a man and wanted his attention or his touch. But here I was, smitten.

He must have felt something similar, or seen what must have been a blush. Certainly my face felt warm. So did my body. He stopped abruptly and looked at me, and Bredon almost ran into him. He seemed to look disbelieving of his own reaction, which thrilled me. Holy cow, I thought, loving that expression even in my mind, holy cow, what just happened? Was it only lust? I was feeling flutters in my stomach and between my legs, lust yes, and desire, its newness and magnitude thrilling me.

My brother, who had just avoided colliding with him, could see the way we were looking at each other, no words sufficient to describe the obvious attraction between us.

"My sister, Dray," Bredon told the man quietly.

"Oh." He was almost flustered, and then, catching himself he said, "I'm Grenville Rand, but everyone just calls me Rand." He grinned, and I recognized the boy he must have been, and understood the decision to avoid the "Grenville." I had been christened Andrea Elizabeth Drayman Cooper. Bredon had called me "Dray" affectionately, when I was a baby, and the name had stuck.

Rand repeated my name, not looking at my brother, only looking at me. Then, as though mentally shaking himself, he began the standard "I'm happy to meet you" phrases, which I mechanically echoed. We were beguiled into silence, just looking at each other, each seeming to feel amazement at the other's existence.

My brother continued to stand quietly beside me, and Rand realized that Bredon was waiting for him to leave. With a lingering look, a soft "Well, good-bye," and a nod to my brother, he went to the waiting elevator. I stole a last look at him as he turned to face the closing doors, and he looked directly back at me in that moment. I was surprised that my usually observant and protective brother made no comment. Evidently Bredon had much on his mind, and my amazement over Rand left me distracted as well. This was a true first for us. Generally, Bredon and I had each other's immediate, complete attention when we were together.

In Bredon's office, after our customary quick hug and a peck on the cheek, we settled into the big armchairs, looking over the city through windows that ran floor to ceiling. I was still thinking of Rand, half in a daydream as I gazed at the familiar scene, listening as my brother started to brief me about his new financial venture. It would be the most exciting deal he had ever put together, and the greatest financial risk of his career.

He had begun in a normal conversational voice, but something he said triggered a buzz of danger and wariness in my unconscious. Thoughts of Rand disappeared as Bredon set out the details of his latest venture. All the years of hearing about the financial world, and all my studies, came together to make me shake my head. I did not like the deal, nor the world regions it involved, nor the overseas partners. It involved enormous investments in countries notorious for their corruption and political instability. The capital partners were mostly men of publicly questionable ethics. The whole project would be dangerous and risky under any circumstances, and conditions now were even less stable. Many observers saw threats of state collapse, coup, revolution, anarchy in the regions that would be part of Bredon's project. I had just finished two semesters of economics that were filled with cautionary tales about many of these regions.

Bredon knew all that I knew, yet he had gone ahead. He was going to deal with men of duplicity and self-interest, feeding government corruption, shattering many hopes among their countries' poor. Each day brought more news of unrest, terrorism, religious and secular upheavals. They affected market performances throughout the world, prices fluctuating in rollercoaster rides, way high up, way down, as investors evaluated each new world development.

No wonder, as Bredon described the investment plan, I was feeling an edgy agitation, alarms stirring in me, and my need to warn my brother. My father always encouraged me to trust my instincts, believing 'instincts' are things we already know within ourselves. Those instincts were now telling me frantically to ask Bredon to pull out of this deal. The profits would be enormous, yes, if it succeeded, but the deal itself was risky beyond anything he had ever tried.

Saying a little prayer to our father's spirit to invoke guidance, I tried to open the conversation gently. "I don't really like this project, Bredon," I said in a low voice, without urgency, praying he would hear my love and care. My words stopped my brother short, surprise in his questioning look. In the past, I might ask questions, but I never questioned his judgment or genius in matters of money. I tried to elaborate. "The principals in the deal...." I began, but Bredon cut me off, his face stern, almost cold.

"You seem to like Rand, and Rand is one of the principals. He had his doubts too, but he'll come around."

"Really? Rand is in it?" I was surprised, and only a bit relieved. "What doubts does he have?"

Bredon shook his head. "Natural caution. But Rand has a major option. He's almost as heavily committed as I am, but we need a tremendous amount more. We need heavy-investment partners in each country we're dealing with."

I felt chilled as my brother spoke, and feared for him. He had to see my face, my "don't do it" face as he called it. This time he was not moved by it, or perhaps it angered him because there was already so much uncertainty in this hugely risky investment. He spoke in a calm but coolly determined voice. "Yes, the other investors are an iffy bunch. But with Rand in the picture, there will be two of us to keep it on course."

I still looked doubtful and Bredon tried another tack. "I know it's huge, a major gamble, and it scares a lot of people. But if we pull it off, the profit will be fantastic."

"It's an enormous gamble, Bredon…" I started to say, but he cut me off.

"I've gambled before," he reminded me.

"Yes. And won. But a gamble is only wonderful if it succeeds." I kept the tone of my voice quiet until then, but my fears for my brother were only growing by the minute. Praying I would sound like my father, I said, "Why not let this one pass?" And then I took a chance and said it: "It almost seems reckless."

"Reckless." Bredon repeated my word without inflection, flat, and with a look of disbelief on his face. Was there also anger? Over this? I had the horrible feeling that engulfs a person when a situation is dangerous to someone you love, but that person will not believe you. There is no persuading them of how likely and how terrible the consequences would be.

"The deal feels too dangerous," I said, keeping my voice calm.

"I've done my homework, Dray," he said in a quiet, remonstrating tone. "You don't trust my judgment?"

"I don't trust the *others*!" I exclaimed. I was feeling a panic for him that I had never felt before, and he could hear it. I wished he would understand that he was the *only* person, and no other, and no thing, that could make me feel this way. After my parents, all my sense of danger centered only on Bredon's well-being. It wasn't just Bredon protecting me. That was what the world saw. I felt a loyalty and desire to keep him from harm, beyond anything I could describe even to myself.

"Bredon," I tried again, "these are not ethical people; they aren't trustworthy. And the political scene is messy, dangerous…"

He cut me off. "I know they're not ethical. That's what contracts are for. If we all 'trusted' each other so much, we could just give our word, and that would be that." My brother shifted impatiently in his chair. "Of course they're out for their own good. But they control access to important permits and contracts. There's no other way than to deal with them."

I was about to answer him but he held up his hand to stop me. "This is business, not friendship, Dray. I've done this kind of deal before."

My brother's voice was so cold, I knew I had lost the argument. He was going ahead with a gamble that could break him, and I knew my brother. If he lost his hold on his financial world, if his losses destroyed his wealth, I was not sure he could endure it. That's what frightened me most of all. Would he feel such shame and humiliation that he would harm himself? Other men had taken their own lives when they were financially ruined. I was terrified at the thought of anything that could take my brother from me.

Bredon seemed to realize the depth of my anxiety, and I began to realize that he could not accept my objections because he probably already committed beyond his ability to get out, even if he wanted to. I could hardly breathe.

"Why not try to get out however you can," I urged, uselessly.

"Of course I could get out," he said, "but I've created this deal, and I'm staying in." He pretended an air of dismissive amusement, patting my hand. I sensed it was a lie, and maybe he was lying to himself. Another first. My sense of menace was so strong, I was so afraid for him, it was all I could do to keep from crying and begging. At this point, though, it was futile and would only add misery to whatever uneasiness he felt. So I tried to compose myself as he took my hand, leaning toward me, his face now loving, all severity gone. And the truth finally there.

"Please, Dray," he said gently, "stop worrying. I'm committed to this. I was just filling you in on the details. No more arguments, please." I knew that tone of voice, all objections done. "And sign the tax form."

He pushed the paper toward me, looking both distracted by

his monster deal, and moved by concern for me. He put his hand on my arm, then gave me a full hug. I loved him so much, and ached because if he lost this gamble, if financial devastation were added to all the loss we had experienced, he would be undone. The damage might be irreparable.

"Please don't worry," he repeated. "And I wish I had more time for you this afternoon, but I have another investor coming in about a half hour." He rose, my sign to rise as well. He tried to assuage my upset and worry, giving me several small kisses on the cheek, trying to change my expression. I finally managed to smile, and gave him another peck on the cheek. It was eerie, how unsettled I felt, how afraid for him. Seeing my worried face, Bredon pressed my arm, hugged me, and gave me a last quick peck on the cheek as the elevator doors opened for me.

"I love you, Baby Sister," he said, and smiled. I melted. I loved him with all the added love I could no longer show our parents. So I gave him a quick hug and another quick peck on the cheek as I stepped into the elevator. Be strong, I told myself. I tried to smile at him all the way to the lobby by smiling upward at the camera hidden behind the elevator's two-way mirror. Each of the suites on these floors had its own mirrored elevator, with invisible as well as visible security cameras. My brother could monitor my progress by looking at a small computer screen at one corner of his desk. I hoped he saw me smiling at him.

The elevators were so fast, I was still smiling upward as the doors opened at ground level. There in the great lobby I saw Rand, smiling back at me. He came up to me quickly.

"I was hoping to see you," he said. "Are you free this afternoon? Do you have some time to spend with me?"

I was so surprised it took me a moment to answer him. Shaking away my disorientation over my brother, gathering my thoughts, I wondered at the fact that Rand had waited here all this time. I was also sensing some relief. Rand would not be waiting for me if he had decided to ditch my brother and back out of the deal. So I said, "Do *you* have the time?" I knew how intensely these men worked, how scheduled their daytime hours.

"I have the time, if you'll say yes," he said softly but flirtingly. "Yes, I do," I said. "The term is over, final exams finished last week." I was close to babbling. I assumed he knew I was a student and my answer was so sensible, but it was all play-acting. It was so exciting just to be near him, his male chemistry making my heart speed up, and my first experience with "butter-flies in the stomach" over a man. I kept trying to look composed, to appear far more cool and proper than I felt.

"There's a Balthus exhibit at the Met," he said, half turning his head to look at me, the question hidden in his statement. "Do you know his work?"

"Yes! He's fascinating!" I replied. Didn't this man understand how nerdy a girl I was? Of course I knew Balthus, with his peculiar and cryptic paintings, girls with their panties showing, legs open as though to invite sex. The picture of the spanking and the breast. As a free-thinking woman I was conflicted over the way he painted women in strange sexual positions. I often wondered why men were not painted that way more often. There were artists who had painted men masturbating, sitting in a chair with their penises in their hands. And Picasso had done a picture of himself on top of one of his mistresses, his penis showing as it neared to entering her. But mostly, men painted their endless fascination with women, breasts and breasts and breasts, and the women with open legs or fully frontally nude, with or without hair on their pubic areas. Balthus painted his model, Thérèse, as a girl, her hairless sex detailed between her open legs.

Thinking these things, I did not realize that Rand was smiling at me the way my professors did when they watched me speculate on something. He was waiting for me to come to a conclusion, as they so often had.

I nodded yes. "Do we need tickets for the exhibit?" I asked.

"No. We can have an early preview."

I would find out what that meant, but now I said innocently, "I have a museum membership," remembering that I had put aside all mail, including probably this exhibit notice from the museum, as I studied for final exams. "I guess the invitation is in a pile of stuff waiting to be read." My look, with its wry shamefacedness, got him to laugh.

"We can go there, and then to dinner. Do you want to?"

Remembering to look cool, and steadying my voice, I said, "Oh, yes, that would be great."

Did I want to? I would have cut two thousand classes and a Nobel lecture for him, the way he aroused me. Not to mention swim the English Channel. Being this close to him, even without touching him, felt so wonderful, and so alarmingly different from anything I had ever felt when I was with a man, I could barely get the words out. "And now that I've met with my brother, I have no more appointments today," I told him. Didn't I sound in charge of myself? Why couldn't I get the fluttering to stop?

As we left the building a uniformed driver got out of a black car and came around to the curb. He gave a kind of half-salute to Rand as he opened the door for us.

"Met Museum, Tom," Rand told him, and then with a quickly mouthed apology he made a short call, after which he said, "Our visit is on."

We got through the heavy afternoon traffic smoothly, crossing from Madison Avenue and turning onto Fifth Avenue just north of the Museum. Tom found his way around the buses and taxis in their special curb lane, to the museum's parking garage in its underground hiddenness. We waited for a pause in the pedestrian traffic so we could cross the pavement onto the garage driveway. I had also used this garage, and knew that cars had to open their trunks for inspection. Oh, the terrible lessons of buildings bombed, as well as planes.

As the parking guard approached us, Tom hit the automatic release and the trunk lifted. The guard thanked him, greeting us with a "Hello, Mr. Rand," did a quick check of the trunk and closed it.

"You're here so often he knows your name." I smiled.

"Yes." His eyes twinkled. "You'll read about it in the Arts section of The Times this Sunday. I'm the newest trustee."

This news excited me even more. It was a major honor to be a museum trustee. "I'm impressed," I said, my admiration unmistakable, causing him to grin in that boyish way I already loved. "You're kind of young for such an honor," I added, though I did not really know how old he was. And I was reluctant to ask him. And I didn't care. But I thought all museum trustees were of matriarch and patriarch age, in charge of family fortunes, guardians of good taste, adding prestige to their family names.

"Family money seems to have done the trick," he said with mock sarcasm. "My father mentioned that he would love to support the museum in a substantial way, but wanted someone he trusted, like his son Rand, on the Board."

"And they agreed...." I marveled.

"They didn't seem to mind," he said, his voice drily humorous. "And it was easier because I went to school with the new Director's brother. Our families have been close friends for years. We also have a pretty valuable art collection of our own." He grinned again and looked at me sidewise. "It also helps that my family has been buying up some of the best newer artists."

I knew Bredon had been doing the same thing, and wondered if they had bid against each other. But none of that mattered. I was so happy to be with Rand, going to a museum I loved, and with one of its trustees! And not a trustee who was old and staid, but a vibrant lion who stirred me wondrously. Aroused by him, I wished I were bolder, wanting to kiss him and touch him. Oh, restraint. I sensed the same commotion in him, though I thought he hid it far better. I used to think I was cold and incapable of this sort of arousal. My whole thinking had changed with his powerful, magnetic personhood, his him-ness, I suppose the Buddhists would call it.

As we left the car Rand told Tom, "I'll phone when we're coming back." A quick walk, through the revolving glass doors of the garage entrance, up the steps. We were in the anteroom of the great downstairs hall, three guards at a desk, alert and watchful, observing visitors. We showed them our membership cards, and seeing Rand's card, they directed us to come behind their desks to get on an elevator that was definitely not for the public.

A guard got in with us, a quick trip upward, and the doors opened onto behind-the-scenes workshops. We were in an area off-limits except to the highly skilled artists and artisans who prepared and restored the priceless works that made the museum a world showpiece. High level museum officials worked diplo-matically but firmly to keep potentially intrusive donors and trustees away from these work areas. The policy was strictly enforced, defended as a safety and security precaution. The donors could do their dance of power, giving to have wings or collections named for them. The museum only cared about provenance, where the works came from, that they were not stolen, or counterfeit. Major museums and various world govern-ments still struggled with these issues, especially of paintings stolen in the Holocaust, art looted during civil wars and insur-gencies. Over the years much stolen art had been returned to rightful owners or their descendants. Still, questions continued to emerge over who owned what, and who had permission to give, to show, and to withhold great works from public view.

There were also collectors who did not want public notice of their holdings, the 'anonymous lenders' listed in exhibit catalogues. Fear of theft, insurance rates, the simple desire for privacy, aversion to publicity that cast light on a family's wealth, all contributed to the desire for anonymity. This Balthus exhibit had quite a few such lenders, I had heard.

So I was even more impressed that we had been admitted to these strictly guarded work areas, and our presence, so unusual, got the workers' attention too. They looked away and went back to their tasks as Rand and I were joined almost immediately by a young woman who introduced herself as the first assistant for this show. With a friendly but professionally neutral expression, she moved us gracefully but quickly through the work area, past the tools of every sort, aprons covering the workers as they did fine restorations, smells of various paints and glues and chemicals which, despite a good, modern air filtering system, had seemed to embed in the walls and flooring.

"Why are we coming in this way?" I whispered to Rand.

"The exhibit opens tomorrow for members only, then in two weeks for the general public. We're going into the exhibit the back way."

"Won't we be noticed?"

"No. The regular entrance is closed, and we're avoiding having to deal with the security locks. But we'll have a guard with us." Rand waved to a uniformed man whom I now saw had been walking behind us. I nodded to the guard, who gave a bare return nod, his demeanor very serious, the sober faced and vigilant behavior I always saw in museum guards. "He's with us for insurance and security's sake, Dray."

I understood the museum's concerns. Art was a thief's precious commodity these days, when surplus cash from great corporations and private fortunes was parked in ever more expensive paintings and antiques. "It's fine," I said, looking back at the guard, "it's as it should be." At which Rand gave me an appreciative look.

The assistant led us to a door, opening it and using a control panel to light the exhibit. "You can begin here, and just loop around," she said. "I'll leave you to enjoy it on your own. Please come back the same way you came in, and the guard will bring you back out."

Rand nodded, and we both thanked her. I was grateful for her polished, unobtrusive guidance, her obvious control over this rare situation. She gave us a pleasant, formal smile and was gone.

Now it was Rand and me, our attentive but discreet guard following behind us, and the surrounding works of the phenomenal artist in all his enigmatic art. I was struck by the paintings and drawings gathered into this show, to see them so close, these originals like a musical vibration that no repro-duction, however fine, could capture. The nearness of Rand was thrilling my body, but so was the art, making me feel overwhelmed with sensation.

The first drawing was before us, the strange threesome; two women with a man. He was leaning against a chair, and I wondered if the man was a Balthus self-portrait. He was looking at the two women. One woman was holding and restraining the other, keeping her from running out the door. Both women had dresses on, but from the prominence of their breasts I thought they might as well be naked. Breasts, breasts, breasts; here it was again. The artist liked high, small, often pointy breasts, and open legs. In the drawings and paintings, the women seemed all to have their legs open.

Next we came to his drawing of a girl presumably getting dressed, but she looked like she was lifting her skirt up, showing her belly, her crotch, her legs, all bare. Does one put on a dress first and *then* put on panties?

I must have said that last question aloud, in my fascination with the interspersed oils and drawings, wonderfully set at eye-level. I caught myself as Rand moved forward to look at me, obviously wondering whether I had been talking to him.

"Thinking out loud," I confessed.

"I would think the underwear goes on first," he said, attempting seriousness and trying not to laugh. And with that, he had all my attention again, warmth returning. The strange and skewed eroticism of the art all around us was making me somehow more aroused by Rand's touch. His arm had come to encircle me, his fantastic cologne a hint on the air as he moved.

We came to the iconic Balthus painting, the young girl Thérèse, her head turned to her right, eyes closed, presumably dreaming, her legs apart, one foot on the floor, the other leg lifted on the stool, her skirt and slip falling back from her thighs, her crotch revealed, narrowly covered by the white panties of a young girl. Beside the stool, beyond her feet and closer to the viewer was the cat, its eyes also closed in the pleasure of the cream it was lapping from the saucer before it. The seated girl looked thoughtful, without shame, indifferent to or unconscious of the artist's gaze. Her head was turned away from him, yes, but also from us. I wondered what she had been thinking.

Next came the most troubling and darkly erotic of the paintings, the guitar lesson. The instrument lay on the floor. The presumptive "teacher" sat in a wide curved-back armchair. Her "pupil" was a girl lying face-up across her lap, her skirt pushed above her navel, naked hips, naked pre-pubescent sex, its lips close together, tight. Her thighs were bare, and she had what looked to me like bruised knees above knee-high white stockings and shoes in place. The teacher's left hand was on the girl's left thigh, as though both holding her and preparing to masturbate her. The teacher's other hand was grasping a handful of the girl's long hair, holding her head down, and the girl was seeking balance by holding her right hand against the floor. She pinched her teacher's exposed naked right breast with her left hand.

This was a stop-in-one's-tracks painting, the girl's jutting hip bones, her flat stomach, and those bruised knees that made me think she had been kneeling in another sexual posture just before now.

I must have been so totally absorbed by the paintings that I seemed to drift into them, the way only such art can do to the viewer. I was undone by this strange genius, each work suggesting so many sexual stories to me as I felt the warmth of my own sexual arousal and desire.

Rand had been watching me. I came back to myself, finding myself leaning ever more tightly against him, excited by the perverse eroticism of this painting, not lewd, but brutal in the way it both drew and repelled me.

"You remind me of her." Rand bent to whisper into my ear, gazing at the painting.

"Not the teacher, I assume," I whispered back, feeling aroused again by his breath and the tone of his whisper, a lover's flirtation.

"Not the teacher," he agreed, his whisper holding laughter.

"Am I as plain as Thérèse, or even Georgette?" I whispered, naming two of the models the artist had used. I wanted to hear Rand flatter and praise me. I wanted him to find me beautiful, I who had always scorned men's come-ons when they complimented my looks. I, who had always dismissed beauty, because the world had found me beautiful. I would say, "I had nothing to do with it. It's genetics, the luck of the draw," my cloak of humility. How cavalier I had been! And now I wanted affirmation, I wanted this man to want me the way my body wanted him. I could hardly think except how sexual desire kept growing in me, and was this my comeuppance for the indifferent way I had treated all the other men who had courted me? What a way to pay for my sins!

"You are *so* not plain," he laughed, "and surely everyone has told you that all your life." A man used to dealing with privileged women, confident. But then he seemed afraid he had offended me and quickly added, "And that's *not* something I'm just saying." Ernest. His arm around me seemed to tighten by microns, but I felt the enclosing sweetness of it.

"*Merci.*" Was I, who was never coy, thanking him in *French*? Was I crazy? Any other time I would have thought, "get hold of yourself." Now I did not care, even if I seemed like a fool in my own eyes. Bimbo-giggly French. Holy cow indeed.

I had no more emotional energy to linger here, and my look told him that I was ready to leave. He steered us back to the entry door, the guard hurrying ahead of us to open it, and then locking it behind him, joining us as we rapidly crossed the workrooms and back to the elevator.

"Let's go out the front way," I told Rand, and the guard, hearing me, pushed the button for the main lobby rather than the garage level. I needed time to cool down after my major internal foray into the wonder of slutty lust. I was still caught by my own reserve, that internal struggle between passion and control that can lead to surrender or to parting.

The elevator door opened in a small recess on the main floor. We thanked the guard for his help, receiving his solemn-faced nod as we exited. We walked, not talking, past the gorgeous Greek statuary and urns, turning to the main lobby. The guards there looked at us quizzically because we did not have the little entry decals on us showing we had formally entered the museum. No one had thought of this, but we passed the guards quickly into the neutral great lobby where you could sit with no decal.

As usual, large numbers of visitors were milling around, some seated on the benches opposite the gift shops, some taking brochures from the slotted outer counter of the great central desk. Within the desk's enclosure were the multi-lingual staff and volunteers for the polyglot crowd visiting New York. The great dinosaur skeletons were across the park on the West Side, but here along Fifth Avenue was "Museum Mile," the Jewish Museum a glory in the upper reaches of the magical area, coming southward to pass the Guggenheim and other breath-stopping landmarks. These were interspersed with embassies and impossibly expensive residences, and concluded with this magnificent museum.

We exited the main doors, descending the steps to Fifth Avenue. Rand had sent some kind of signal to Tom, because he stood waiting outside Rand's car at the curb beneath us. The day was too beautiful and my body too heated and wild for me to want to be driven anywhere just yet. The late afternoon breeze made the air sweet and bright and cool. The beauty of the coming evening, Rand's scent, and my new-found lust for a man, so surprising and wonderful, made me reluctant to do anything but be with him.

I was thinking, I wish he would kiss me, embrace me, I want to kiss him, where did this come from; I was lost in my heat and happiness. Outwardly I still drew upon the disciplined manners I had learned long ago but my body had its own agenda. Heat traveled from my navel downward, and it was all I could do not to touch myself, to feel whether that heat was coming through my panties, whether I would feel the pulsing of desire with my hand. Unthinkingly I had started walking south, along the Park wall, and Rand fell into step beside me, signaling Tom who jumped back into the car and managed, in all the traffic, to trawl slowly behind us, watching us, pacing the car to our steps.

"I live downtown," Rand said, "on the East Side. We could eat there. Will you have some dinner with me?" He took my hand gently as he asked, producing another surge of chemistry and heat. I could not really speak, afraid I would squeak or sob or I-don't-know-what, so I just nodded and he was openly pleased, his response making him look very young, the boy he had been flashing once more into the face of the man he was now.

It was so nice to see this reaction, a man's frank pleasure not hidden by the mask of jaded sophistication that people in our circles so often assumed. In the often crazy social life of the rich and powerful, some people thought that if they took open pleasure in being with you, it would give you a kind of power over them. So boring, so soulless. Rand was so refreshing, not hiding the happiness he felt.

At Rand's signal, Tom pulled the car to the curb and we settled into the familiar cushioned leather comfort of the back seat. My body thrilled as he slid in beside me and moved closer to me while the car pulled out into the thick but moving traffic.

Turning to face me, seeing my eyes and seeming to sense my breath, Rand drew me against him and slowly covered my lips with his. I thought I would catch fire and I could feel his own flush of heat. He drew away looking at me speculatively, delightedly, hardly believing it either, it seemed. I thought, such magic. He hesitated just for a few seconds, then drew me to him again, a long kiss that had my blood so throbbing, it was like orgasm, everything a haze of pleasure.

Oh, this was so not me! I who had played indifferently with boys, preferring dancing, studying, swimming, touring, hating the thought of the casual hook-ups so many of my peers seemed to enjoy. I had kept my distance from the frantic games of petting and maneuvering for sex, and the search games online and off, of "where is my boyfriend now," with all its pointless jealousies. No great loves had been created that way, at least, not that I could see. So many of the boys, and the girls too, were pompous, full of their supposed worldliness and sophistication. It was a total lie. I could not see or feel any richness or specialness in their frantic pairings and partings. I avoided most of that "social life." My peers and our wider circle of friends and their families, assumed that this was due to my continuing trauma over my parents' unspeakable deaths. That suited me. It gave me the space I needed from sexual routines and rituals that were, to me, no life at all.

Among all my peers, I was closest to one of my classmates, she and I having found each other the first week of our just-ended freshman year. Each of us was an outlier, different from our classmates despite the great diversity of the women admitted to each college class. We had found in each other someone to confide in and laugh with, the essential other female each of us seems to need or long for, to share our commentary on the world. Her name was Robin, and I told her when we met that she was named for my favorite bird. She told me drily that she was named for her grandmother, and that was our first great laugh together. She and I shared a mocking despair over the impossibility of most of the young men about us.

The boys I had really liked until now were as shy as I was, and the sexual exploring we had done had not really roused me beyond curiosity and some clumsy experimenting. Still, I had done enough so that I was not exactly a virgin, although there had not yet been any sex that swept me away. Until now. And this wasn't even sex, I didn't think, at least, not yet.

But even if this, with Rand, wasn't sex, I was still ready to collapse into a sensual heap after his two kisses, the last one so long and wonderful that I would not have cared if that were my final moment on earth. I loved it.

The car pulled to the curb in front of a great luxury apartment building, old-fashioned in its brown stonework and broad shoulders, unlike the sleek towers in other parts of the city. I knew this area. Bredon had lived just north of here briefly, before buying the penthouse further uptown where he now lived.

I managed an empty-headed phrase in a voice that did not shake too much. "Your apartment is here?" Of course it was. We surveyed the rich exclamation point of the entrance canopy at one side. A discreet carriage drive circled the other side of the long front of this massive edifice, whose quiet stone calmly hid all the great wealth of its interior.

"My family management corporation owns this building," he said quietly, as we got out of the car. He was amused that I obviously did not know how rich and important he was. But I did know that his was one of the player families in the great economic scrambling and dueling of the city and its overseas connections. It all seemed so unimportant as long as he might give me another of those kisses, though my knees would probably buckle if he tried it right now.

Tom made sure we were well clear of the car before he drove

it away, probably to the judiciously hidden garage at the side of the building, entrance by special radio code. The rich often hide their opulence under bland or unseen entrances, a way to avoid the envious, the stalkers, the protesters, the criminals who would rob or even kidnap. My brother had shown me all the secret ways to seem to disappear in a car into the side of a building like this, and enter the interior with its great inner courtyard open to the sky, a mini-city of affluence guarded by the concierge, doormen, porters, and quiet but stern security men in plain suits. To newcomers, the security men looked like visitors waiting for someone to come join them.

"Would you like to come in?" he asked. And then, unexpectedly shy, he said, "Or would you rather we just went to dinner?"

I did not know if he had some strange moral code about women – you never knew what played in men's minds, especially rich men who could have women at will, or who could have their fantasies played out for a fee. I was not naïve about such things. Rand seemed to have escaped that Freudian morass, or at least he *seemed* to be free of it. But I had not yet even asked him *the* critical question. "Are you married?" I blurted.

"No!" He almost boomed the answer, laughing now. "And I haven't been."

More relief. No baggage – I hoped – of ex-wives and step-kids, re-wiring each other's psyches into knots of love, deprivation, hurt, cruelty, or depression. Lately the rich were more likely than even middle class people to marry, to marry later, to stay married and have a couple of kids who then became their obsession. This is what I saw among the longtime richer people; it might be the future even for Bredon and his fiancée. Maybe it was different for the newer rich people, as it was for the celebrities, new to luxury, tempted by all the things that destroy, especially alcohol, especially drugs.

Rand went back to my question. "Were you burned by dating

a married man?" he asked.

"No. Married guys are bad karma," I replied. I had seen enough girls believing a married man was actually going to leave his wife for them. Some of my classmates had fallen for predatory professors. One was especially notorious. I told Rand about him, how every new graduating class had its "Professor Burns Alumnae," women who had been "this year's" mistresses. Every one of them thought she was, at last, "the one," who would have him for herself. He preyed on beautiful, needy young women; the grifter and the predator know their targets. I had called his lovers "Burned Women," angrily, for he had made a try for me, to my immediately obvious horror, and he withdrew as though *he* had been burned by the way I looked at him. The remembrance made me shiver and Rand looked at me with a sad smile, but said nothing. I wondered how many times he had heard similar stories. Every woman has at least one story.

We had resumed our southward walking, this time for a short distance and had almost reached the end of the block. A small narrow building sat there, incongruously, with old-fashioned steps and a neat canopy of its own, showing a dimly lit vestibule.

"Here we are," Rand said, taking my arm and guiding me up the three brownstone-type steps. As we passed through the door into what I thought would be darkness, we were at the entrance of an elegant little jewel of a restaurant, all glistening linen and the glint of silverware. "This is our corner pub and fast food eatery," he teased me as the impeccable maître d' approached us.

"Monsieur Rand," he said, giving me the swiftest, briefest glance, seeing everything. I was filled with admiration at his smooth, quiet authority. "Will there be any more guests?" he asked in a very low voice.

"Just the two of us," Rand told him, and he immediately turned to lead us to a table. There were two other couples already dining, their conversation soft, sound hardly carrying.

I let Rand order for us, a quick, delicious, efficiently served dinner, and I ate between surges of between-the-legs heat as he rested two fingers on the back of my hand. He could not touch me enough. I was making disconnected small talk about college, so glad the term was over. He said little except an encouraging "did your exams go well?" to my nodding "yes," and I was mining my scarce experience with boys and sex to figure out how I could make love to him, wondering if he would see me as a slut, not caring, desire driving me. I ate enough to quell the hunger pangs that had risen up when the plate was set before me, but my appetite was for him, and I was madly controlling my impatience.

I looked at the diners around us, being seated, eating, leaving. No one seemed to pay a check; another couple had left by simply putting down their forks, rising from the table and exiting.

"All private accounts," I commented, trying to find something that would distract me from wanting to be done with dinner and melt into him.

"Yes." He nodded. "It's like a private dining room for the building. Did you enjoy it?"

"It's fabulous." It was. Fusion cooking, simple, elegant, and a glass of wine that was perfect. The alcohol was illegal for me in New York, where the drinking age is twenty-one. But no one ever questioned me about my age in the restaurants I had been to with my parents and then with Bredon. After I was sixteen, my parents allowed me to have wine at dinner, just as it was allowed in public in Europe. When I was not with family, I drank mineral water or plain water or iced tea, it made no difference to me.

I saw that Bredon was done and waiting for me. I quickly put my fork and knife down on the plate, rising as he did. The maître d' gave him a discreet nod as we left.

I was so happy to be walking with him again, going toward the end of the long block. His arm was now fully around me, and he carefully placed a small kiss above my ear. I was controlling a moan from that little kiss for it was like a miniature fire-dart making me even warmer. His breath was a bit ragged, so I knew, finally, that he was feeling what I felt, only he was so much better at control. Well, he was older. I could not get my thoughts straight to figure how much older. Not as old as my brother. Maybe thirty. My body did not care.

"I'll show you where I really live," he whispered as he planted little kisses down my hairline, and I feared that if we did not get there soon, he was going to have to hold me up. We turned the corner, and there extending behind the buildings was a tiny gated park. He pulled a small remote from his pocket and the gate unlocked with a soft click. He guided me through and let it close and lock behind us as he moved me down a flat stone path. Above us were great blank back walls of the apartment buildings. We turned behind a small line of trees, and there was an exquisite brownstone, a survivor perhaps from an earlier era in New York, hidden by the tall buildings behind it, and hidden from the street by the trees and bushes that blocked any real view beyond the gate.

It was not the typical brownstone with the long stone flight of stairs and basement stairwell. The first floor was at ground level, with a direct entrance off the path, small lights cleverly placed and shaded to guide us without being visible from anywhere else. Another remote command and the front door unlocked. With our quick entry the door closed behind us, another barely audible click, and low lights discreetly set in the corners came on with a soft glow. It was a sitting room, filled with charm and smelling fresh, frankincense and flowers perfuming the air, the actual flowers in two vases, gorgeous, fragrant. There was a fireplace against the far wall, a shining brass screen between the andirons. He led me directly to the great enveloping sofa, removing his jacket as he lowered me onto the wonderful cushions. He was running his hands over my body.

"My God," he breathed, the words hardly audible, "what breasts," and then his hand slipping under my skirt, quickly finding me, hot, wet, and the movement of his fingers and hand brought me a rushing climax that startled me as it happened. He could feel it, and I would swear that he chortled at his triumph, his ability to have this limp and melted young woman beneath his body, then one hand unbuttoning his shirt, then both his hands pulling my panties downward, and I ran my hand over his formidable erection.

I decided to try the ancient technique that Robin and I had learned by accident, from a wonderful woman, a classmate's mother, who was a sex therapist. We called her "Mrs. Sanjay" because the couple's last name had been difficult for Sara's teachers. (Sara's full name was Saraswati, whom I considered a super-goddess, but that name too was a non-starter for English-bound teachers and classmates.) Sara had forgotten that we were coming to her apartment to get her for a day of galleries and bookstore browsing, but Mrs. Sanjay was so gracious, she had had the maid bring tea and cakes, as though we were visiting *her* on an afternoon in India. The print on the wall facing us was both exotic and erotic, and in answer to our eager questions about it, she teasingly, gently, explained some of the ways of pleasure that the print illustrated. We listened in excited fascination, and afterwards promised each other that we *had* to try these things as soon as possible. Alas, thus far, no boy had suited me, and when Robin had tried it, the boy was so shocked he practically ran away from her. We laughed and screamed over that, and it was a warning to both of us that the double standard still dwelt in the minds of men, no way to know which of them held onto it.

But here was Rand, perfect for my great experiment. He was not circumcised, which surprised me, but I would find out why some other time. Now, I took his penis in my hand, slipping the foreskin back, the inner shaft viscous and hot as I passed it into my cupped palm, then running its tip on the horizontal line across the palm, and I could hear him gasp.

"What are you doing?" he managed to ask, consumed. But I

only gazed up at the ceiling with a little smile, hotter than ever at his ecstasy. Mrs. Sanjay had explained that this action would not make him come. He would have to do "the work of that final wondrous completion" himself, as she explained it, but he would find the sex act, as she called it, wildly more pleasurable.

It worked. He was hot as a lion, breathing like some combination of dragon and engine, and I was shivering as he got ready to enter me. I began snaking my arms around him, we were kissing so hotly, he was nibbling my lips and then flitting his tongue over them, so that the world was invisible through a cloud of scent and heat and the sweet downy hair of his chest and around his sex. I held my breath, preparing for what I knew would be a more serious thrust than I had known, and he was against me, about to press into me, and then...

Oh no, oh God, a sound from his jacket, and his blind shock at hearing it, a groan of his pain and frustration, a struggle not to hear it, and almost a small scream at its insistence. Rand kissed my lips and then my neck and pulled his trousers up as he slid away to get the signaling cellphone.

Practically shaking with anger and the aftermath of frustrated passion, he clicked and listened, saying nothing, but as I watched, his eyes changed to a harder focus. I knew that look. We were done.

He clicked off and came to hold me. "I'm so sorry," he said, half panting the words, anger and resignation on his face, seeing my sorrowful and shocked face, my own resignation matching his. I knew he had a major role in his family's high-powered financial dealings, and had seen enough of this world to know what was calling him away. I also recognized how unusual the ringtone had been. Bredon and I had a special emergency ringtone between us. Obviously, something major had occurred, the ringtone signaling an urgent situation, urgent enough even to stop a passion that was making us blind with desire. This was the world we both lived in. To remain rich in a world of high risk and high gain, one had to be vigilant. And that required choices, especially in a world of shifting economies in different time zones. Between love's demands and maintaining one's fortune, the choices were seen as obvious, because it was also assumed but oh-so-politely unsaid, that where fortunes faded away, so did love.

"I must go, Dray, I am so sorry." He said it anxiously, hoping I would not be furious with him. "I'll be back tomorrow night, or I hope by Wednesday. Say we can see each other then."

"Yes," I managed to say; there was nothing for it. He quickly reached for me again, his fingers finding me, his hand working me quickly, so that I climaxed in a hot rush, and he kept his hand hard against me as I throbbed, a pain and pleasure that would have to do for now, though it made me want more.

I didn't even think of his satisfaction, I didn't think to look at him as he did his trousers up and straightened himself out. Only later I realized that I didn't know enough to ask or look. And anyway, I wouldn't have known what I was looking for, whether he would still have his erection, whether it had gone away. I knew the textbooks, but he had the "hands on" experience, my thoughts said wryly. My own real experience was still lacking. He didn't seem to mind. He was so concerned for me, so tender, and so exasperated with fate, I wanted to cling to him and keep him from going anywhere.

As we put our clothes into some presentable semblance of their original neatness, he entered another set of numbers into his phone. I realized that these numbers signaled Tom, for as we left the park, hearing the gate close behind us, we could see him standing by the car, holding the door open.

"I wish I could see you home," Rand whispered, "but you'll be safe with Tom." Rand practically lowered me bodily onto the seat, his last quick kiss on my lips leaving my knees even more shaky, and grateful for his incredible tenderness.

The car took me home in silent luxury, and though I wanted

to cry, I felt drained, wanting the sleep that we should have shared after he had built me up to that crashing pleasure. When I got to my bed, I barely got my clothes off, got under the coverlet, crawled to the center of the bed, and fell into the deepest sleep I had ever known.

IV

When I woke, for the first time in my life I was a creature rumpled from lovemaking, yesterday's clothing all askew around my body.

My normal waking time, when my body roused itself with no alarm, was generally at dawn, even before dawn in winter months. My mother had laughed that I was the only adolescent who naturally rose early. The other side of this was that I also tended to get sleepy early, which did not help my patchy social life. When galas were held, opera openings, ballet festivals, anything lasting into the night, when I attended with my family and was expected to be part of the social display, it was a challenge for me. I would drink several cups of coffee over the course of the day, to charge my body awake at least until midnight. It helped that I was so young, able to coax myself to later hours. I often was going home, or already home, while my peers were madly partying in their after-hours times together. It must have been some sort of relief for my parents, but they did not make a great deal out of it, perhaps afraid to jinx it. They liked what one of my friends called my "lady monk" ways. I was never at a late party. My peers often teased that I was a sleepyhead, but gave up trying to change my stubbornly daylight-oriented body clock. They named me "Cinderella," and called to me that my midnight hour was fast approaching. This would start around ten PM, which was about how late I could hold out before getting into the family car to be driven home. Our driver was the envy of the other drivers, who had to wait all hours for their young charges to make their raucous ways back to their cars.

One time, when I was talking about my friends' exasperation with my inability to stay up late, my mother had said that as I got older, "when you are as old as I am," she had laughed, early nights would be a delicious blessing. Her eyes had been filled with mischief, sympathy for my childish sleeping hours, happiness that I was safely home when others my age were who-knew-where. My mother's eyes shone that way now in my memory. How I missed her, the familiar involuntary sob at the memory of her face, the tears gathering and burning my eyelids, oh, my mother.

I waited to gather myself to some calmer state, and turned to look at the clock. It said eight AM. I was stunned. How late had I returned? And why was I so slow in getting out of bed? Generally, I was totally awake the minute my eyes opened. What had last night done to me? I smiled to myself at my question, suddenly aware of the most gorgeous scent of roses wafting about me. On my desk in the alcove beyond my bed was a vase of red roses, so heavily, headily wonderful, they were like the roses I had seen and adored in India. I had not smelled such roses since, though I always tried to recapture their beauty with my rose perfumes.

A knock at the door, and a little bell. It was Marilisa, the "upstairs concierge" as we called her, the organizer for a cluster of apartments, getting cleaners in and out, accepting deliveries, sending out orders, smoothing life in ways too numerous to list. I managed to say "Come in," and ran into my closet-dressing room, trying to get out of my rumpled clothes and into a robe.

"Good morning," she said cheerily after letting herself in. "The roses smell wonderful."

"Did you...?" Of course she had, her merriment saying yes, she had brought the roses here while I slept.

"They arrived before dawn," Marilisa said. "The concierge couldn't get over their fragrance." She looked at me questioningly. "Where did he buy them?"

"You know it's a 'he,'" I said with a smile.

"Of *course* it's a 'he.' It's traditional to send roses..." She stopped, and now it was her turn to blush.

"I don't know where," I said, but I suspected he had done some extraordinary magic with the international flower marketers. These roses were the essence of India.

"If you find out, I must know," she said. "They are so incredible." And then she looked at me, suppressing a wider smile. "Can I do anything for you?"

"No, thanks Marilisa." I realized that she had seen me asleep in my clothes, and I left her to her imaginings.

"Okay, call if you need me," she trilled on her way out. Her work here was her dream job in many ways, and she was very well paid. The man who had arranged all this for her was, yes, Bredon. She was in love with him and in awe of him, so clear from her reactions the few times I had seen them in the same room. Thus I was her special charge. Bredon had picked well. She was wonderful.

I went and enclosed the vase in my arms, inhaling the fragrance of the roses. The traditional small white envelope sat amid the stems, which had been stripped of their thorns. High-end florists did this routinely, as I had seen, with a small stem-hugging collar that clamped under the blossom; pulling the collar straight down, the thorns came off in a shower. The art was to take the thorns but leave the stems looking green and untouched. There is an art to everything, I thought. Especially love.

Rand's note in the envelope said, "Soon, my Darling. R." And I marveled again at how he had managed to send these, wondering if he had flown to India. I would ask him when he got back, when I thanked him with words and kisses and my body... I was growing heated just imagining it.

A message light blinked; Robin's voice. "Dray, I'm in town passing through, quick lunch? Call me if you can meet me."

I hit the return-redial. "Yes, yes," I said, still half crumpled, my robe not fully on; I was so happy she was back, even for a day.

She laughed at my eagerness. "I can't wait to see you either. First we visited my mother's family. Now we fly out to visit my father's family. Then I can return to the city and live a normal life. I think." Her dry, resigned recitation of her duties had me giggling. But then she grew serious. "I shouldn't be so cavalier," she said. "I *hope* I'm coming back here in two weeks or so. It's open-ended."

"Are you worried? What's happening?" I asked.

"The health of the oldest members of both families is iffy," she replied. "I'm hoping they hang in there. But I don't want to be too definite about it. You know the old saying, if you want to make God laugh, tell Him your plans for the future."

"Or you can tell *Her*. Maybe She'll be more understanding," which got an appreciative chuckle from Robin.

"I'll pick you up and we can eat near your place, okay? We'll have maybe an hour, and then I'm off to the airport."

"Yes, come up," I urged, wanting to share the glorious roses and news of Rand with her.

She knew immediately that something was afoot. "You want me to come to your *apartment* to get you?" she enunciated, and at my giggle she said, "Oooh, now I really can't wait. Noon. See you then," to my laughing, "yes, yes," and I felt that happiness of a best friend coming to share news and heart secrets.

I finally got myself into the shower, and into another set of clothes, rushing now so that if Robin did have more time, we could sit here while I told her about Rand. I turned on my computer, did a cursory scan of my e-mails, nothing pressing, and closed down. I also buzzed down to Marilisa, whose cleaning policy for my apartment and a couple of others, were based on shipboard practices: continual attention, and cleanup whenever needed. I was neat and tidy, but nothing could hide the mess I had made of my bed, the sheets and the coverlet, and she had the changes of bedding for me in her storage closet. All I had to say was, "Marilisa, my bed..." and she said, "I'll be right up."

She and I, on either side of the bed, quickly put on new sheets and a new coverlet. She did the pillowcases, and I retrieved my Watch Bear, a ridiculously menacing stuffed animal over a foot high, that was my appointed sleep guardian. I had brought him to the Blessing of the Animals last year, finding many people with their own little accumulations of toy critters. The priests at Saint Mary's smiled a lot, but never said a word, blessing all the pets, and blessing pictures of beloved animal companions who had died. I was determined to find a special medal for my Bear, to pin it on him, his own talisman, as he was mine.

Marilisa did a quick sweep of the bathroom, gathering towels against my protests, "They're still clean," looking at me with a sly smile, I think not trusting that post-lovemaking towels could be used again. With quick efficiency fresh towels went onto the racks, and she was out the door with a wave at my thanks.

As I had hoped, Robin did arrive a little bit early – maybe fifteen minutes – a bonus of time for us. We hugged briefly as we murmured our hellos, and I stood back to admire her very high heels.

"Five inches!" I exclaimed. "I can't wear them! Are they comfortable?" I was amazed that she had bought such shoes.

"Yes, I bought them for our outings!" she announced solemnly. "I am so tired of neck strain when we walk together."

"Robin, for heaven's sake, I'm just a bit taller than average."

"And I'm a bit shorter, and you're not just a 'bit' taller. In my next life, please God let me be tall!" She sat in one of the small upholstered chairs in my bedroom, inhaling deeply, "And please, God, let someone send me roses like that! Who is it? Who?" She was practically bouncing on the seat as she asked me.

"Rand...." I began.

"*Grenville* Rand? Oh, my God!" She was excited and eager. "Tell me, what happened, did you, did he...."

"It was wonderful." I sat across from her; we were bending toward each other in our excitement. "We went to the Balthus exhibit, and he's going to be a museum trustee, and then we went to dinner, and then to his place, not his apartment..." The words tumbled one on top of the other, yet she and I could hear each other's thoughts as well as our words, and she understood everything.

"Did you?" she asked, giggling.

"Oh, Robin, we never actually got to it! We were, you know, 'in the throes of love,' as they say, and I did Mrs. Sanjay's technique, and he loved it," at which Robin squeaked, her special sound, and bounced on the chair some more. "But just as we were about to, just at the point, his phone rang..." and I never finished the sentence because Robin screeched out an "eeeeek, oh noooooo..."

She was suddenly serious and angry for me. "And he *answered* it?" She was indignant. "Why didn't he just ignore it!"

"You should have heard the weird ringtone, Robin. That was no regular call, and sure enough, he sent me home in his car and flew off, I think late last night, maybe to India since that's the only place I've ever smelled roses like this." I hesitated. "I wonder how he got them here overnight, though..."

"Never mind that!" Robin exclaimed. "You're going to see him again!"

"Yes! I can't believe how he affects me, he's bright and tender and..." I had no more words, I just turned my hands up, surrendering the struggle to describe it.

"And *super* rich!" She looked at me. "Do you know how rich he is?"

"Robin, we're not exactly poor."

"Oooh, but the Rands and the Grenvilles and the Strellings and all the rest of that family are really what 'super' means when they say 'super-rich'." She looked at me with a grin, and said, "I'll bet you haven't Googled him."

"No." It hadn't occurred to me.

"Do you know how many guys have Googled *you*?" she said,

"and me, before or right after we meet?"

"I know people do it..."

"Yes, you innocent creature, I know *you* don't." She was laughing.

"I'm not an innocent creature. Rand wasn't the first man to kiss me or to get to third base."

"Whoever got to third base with you, probably was called out at home." She was still laughing.

"Well, I'm not naïve."

"No, that you're not. You're more clever than most people can ever imagine."

"You're the same," I told her.

"Yes." She was. It was not arrogance. It was a simple statement of fact, and it reflected our sameness.

As we started to leave my apartment she turned back one more to inhale the roses' perfume, lingering over them with a long, dreamy look. Then we were talking as we made our way down to the street and across to a wonderful small café.

Robin was serious now, our earlier conversation evidently very much at play in her mind. "We *are* smart, Dray, and as they say, 'clever beyond our years.' We hide it well, but we know ourselves."

I looked at my friend at she spoke, seeing that she was talking as much to herself as to me, using our familiar pattern of saying our thoughts out loud to each other, no answer needed, but comments lovingly received when one of us did answer.

She went on, "We're at a top school, we've gone to the best schools, and no one puts it together, that all this education may actually have 'taken', and that we're very intelligent, and maybe not wise, but we *know* stuff, and we can think and analyze."

I wondered if my friend had been getting some "get married and be a good wife" lectures from the oldest members of her mother's clan. She was on the way to another set of lectures from the great- and great-great aunts in her father's family. Robin was an heiress-in-the-making, major monies coming to her from both families. For the oldest in these families, the imperative was to keep the family money safe by making a solid marriage and producing a healthy crop of progeny. I had seen a little bit of it, but my family's situation was different. Our parents' families had had very bad luck with health issues. Not many remained of our parents' extended families, and Bredon and I were clucked over in absentia. Our relatives knew that we were a brother and sister more like Lazarus than like Adam, risen from too stark a knowledge of death, not siblings who were young and newly-made. Our relatives also lived mostly at a distance, though we did have a couple of great-aunts in the New York region, who had been a refuge for me after the bombing. Bredon and I, along with some great-cousins, had dutifully visited them these past Christmases and Easters. No one expected us to be there with light hearts, and I blessed the two ancient ladies for their generous love.

Robin had been silent, allowing my own thoughts to wander. Our companionable togetherness was always this way. Just sitting together, just walking together, without words, warming and wonderful. But now Robin came back to her theme with a restless gesture.

"I don't think, even now, even with all that women have achieved, that people really believe how deeply smart we are." She gave me one of her calculating looks. "I wonder if even Grenville Rand, currently the major brain of his family's empire, knows how smart you are." Her expression was dead serious.

"We've only just met, Robin!" I wondered at her steady look, the thoughtful way in which she studied me. "You have reservations about him? Tell me," I said.

"I don't know what it is, Dray. I've seen pictures of him, he's handsome enough."

"Pictures? Where?" Why hadn't I seen them?

"You don't follow what they call 'society gossip'," she said.

Her tone softened. "You've kind of had other things on your mind."

She was right, this insightful friend, how well she knew me. My sense of the proportion of things had shifted, the whole planet had shifted for me, what mattered and what didn't, everything had different weight now. "So tell me the gossip," I said.

"There isn't much, just a couple of pictures. He and his family seem to be as camera-shy as your family, even from before..." She looked down, feeling she had been clumsy in what she said.

I did not want her to feel clumsy. What she said was the truth, and I quickly said, "You're right about my family, and me and Bredon, yes, but I didn't realize that Rand was that way too." I thought for a minute. "I'm glad about it. And he said he was never married, I asked him. Did he have a steady girlfriend?" I hesitated, and then asked, with a flutter of wariness and hope, "Is he linked with anyone now?"

"Lots of women would *like* to be linked with him, but no, no one name," Robin said. She grinned at me, glad to have some good news.

Time was running on. Her family's car and driver were across the street; the driver was now out of the car, waiting, and we knew our precious time together was done. We had a quick argument over who was treating whom, which she won, "Since we're celebrating an almost-there affair," which made me laugh, we hurried across the avenue, thankful for a lull in the endless city traffic. Today, even the killer bicyclists and truck drivers and speeding cars seemed to have found another place to be.

"Have a good trip, Robin," I said, hugging her, missing her terribly even as I held her in a good-bye. "Be safe. Come home soon."

"You're the best, you know." She grinned, and gave me a quick little kiss on the cheek before gracefully folding herself into the familiar back seat, just like Rand's car, just like Bredon's. I stepped back so that her driver could close the door, and I nodded and smiled at him, wanting to say, "Take care of my friend, drive safely," but he saw the look, acknowledging it with a serious nod. I bent and waved good-bye to Robin and stood at the curb watching her car disappear onto the eastbound street, to the highway and the bridge and the roads to Kennedy Airport. I sighed, missing her company and Rand's. I would have to call Bredon and see if he would have dinner with me. I missed my friend, I missed my lover, but I always and forever missed Bredon.

I found my phone when I got back to my apartment, not having missed it while I was with Robin. I was always forgetting or leaving it. Somehow I had escaped the compulsion that sent my generation into a digital day, electronics for every task. Still, I was grateful for the instant connection my phone gave me to Bredon and all who mattered to me.

I started to press the quick dial for Bredon but saw a text waiting. Clicking on it, I read, "Tomorrow night, Darling. R." I was feeling joyful. Rand would be back, and this afternoon I would run to get my hair streaked some more, to look fashionably brown-and-blonde, and maybe indulge in a whole spa treatment. I called Bredon, who quickly agreed to dinner at seven thirty, late for me, but I had to leave time for the spa. I told him I would come get him at his office, since the spa was nearby. He seemed distracted, but there was that major deal going on that undoubtedly had his attention.

Tomorrow I would go looking for what I never bought: the sexy-frilly underwire bras with matching panties that set fantasies in motion. I hoped Rand would be even more excited when he saw them. On Monday night I had on only the basic white underclothing I always wore, nothing fancy, very comfortable. Now I had a reason to buy at the store most famed for sexy underwear – and I would look for the thigh-high stockings that would leave my panties free to be pulled away easily. I sighed, thinking of it, growing warmer, thinking maybe it was time to buy some sex toys to satisfy me when I started thinking of Rand, and giggled to myself at the thought. Tonight I would have to pleasure myself into sleep, images of Rand to drive all my desires.

V

By seven-thirty when I arrived at Bredon's office, I was glowing from a facial, my nails and toes were done, my hair sleekly shaped and falling freely for a change. I was wearing a chic dress and matching sweater-shawl in a pale green that favored my hazel eyes. Bredon had our mother's dark hair and eyes, while I had our father's brown hair and lighter eyes. Yet our faces were similar. No one could doubt that we were brother and sister, and people often commented on how much we looked alike.

I anticipated a compliment, a twinkle, some happiness when Bredon saw that I had made myself glamorous. But all my happy humor faded as I walked out of the elevator and saw Mrs. Andrews standing there, waiting for me.

Her tension was obvious to me even through her habitual formal posture. She gave me that special look that I had first seen three years before, the look that great-souled, loving women give to motherless girls. That look could undo me at first, so that I had to teach myself the painful control that little boys learned, not to cry. The first time I did it, the pain wracked my body, and I understood what so many boys forgot as they grew into men, they forgot the pain of suppressing their tears. For men, the disappearance of that memory seemed unimportant, since the important thing was not to cry, not to be weak, not to be a girl.

That control over my tears had become autonomic, where the body seems to act on its own. I felt that reaction now, steeling myself as I saw Mrs. Andrews' loving and concerned look. But drawing closer to her, I also saw a concern larger than her compassion for me. Bredon. When our parents were lost, she had turned herself into his mother too. This never-married woman, very private, very formal and businesslike, the perfect front desk person for Bredon's office, was transformed by our profound despair, her love for us hidden except to our discerning eyes.

The look on her face had to mean that Bredon was facing trouble. I had never seen this look before, but I sure did know it now, seeing it this first time. I felt a shudder and my stomach felt queasy. Oh God, I prayed, my brother, my brother. Those were the only words of prayer I could think of, but I was sure that God was listening with a compassion infinitely beyond even that of the loving Mrs. Andrews.

Bredon came out of his office with a crisp step, his posture erect, his appearance impeccable. He kissed my cheek and gave me a quick look of admiring appraisal, but I could see that he had much on his mind. When I saw his face, I realized that we should have met at his apartment or mine, to have a serious talk.

"Thanks so much for staying, Mrs. Andrews," my brother told her, his warm tone seeming to ease her heart a bit.

"Yes, thank you," I added, smiling at her, pretending I realized nothing.

She took her cue, nodded her "good-nights," and disappeared into the elevator. Once the doors had closed I asked Bredon, "Would you rather we just went home and talked?" It would be his choice of "home."

"No, Dray, it's all right. I've made reservations; the car is downstairs, let's get something to eat."

We said little to each other on the way to the restaurant, except for Bredon's compliments for what the spa had managed to do to make me shine. The worst of the traffic had passed and we got to the restaurant quickly.

Happily it was a week night, and although Bredon's was a known face among the city's financial and cultural notables, this little restaurant knew how to arrange quiet, private seating, keeping the lights low. Bredon also favored this place because he – and I too – hated the banging about of dishes and doors in busy, less exclusive kitchens. In this restaurant, clatter and noise could get a bus boy or any staff member fired, and tips were too good to let carelessness cost them their jobs. The restaurant was called "La Reine Tranquille," The Tranquil Queen, for a reason. It was a place for quiet dining, low voices, and almost invisible table service.

Bredon's appearance at the restaurant caused the usual quiet stir among the staff, the chef peeking out to wave at him, an order quickly given, wine ordered and poured. Once done, the staff disappeared, knowing not to keep coming to the table while we were talking. No asking, "Is everything all right?" or the other nonsensical and interfering things that wait staff were taught to do in most restaurants. One of the staff always kept an eye on Bredon, but from a respectful distance. If something was not right, Bredon's expression would tell them soon enough.

I was almost afraid to start our conversation, feeling my brother's preoccupation with what had to be heavy news about his big gamble. When I made the dinner date, I had wanted to tell Bredon that I was mad about Rand, that I was going to see him tomorrow, that I had seen Robin, and all my large and small news. Instead I focused on Bredon, his air of distraction stirring fear in my heart.

"Bredon…" I began, and my questions did not need to be asked.

"Well, Dray, you were right in so many ways," he said quietly, with a stoicism so different from anything I had seen before.

"Rand?" I said his name as a question.

"He's coming back from India in the morning." My brother looked at me with sadness and seriousness. "I know you like him, Dray, but he and I have been in the worst possible arguments. His family had a major scare with their investments in India, but he got things set right again."

I waited, taking a token sip of my wine, watching my brother as he seemed to think out loud, talking without really seeing me. "Rand is always pulling rabbits out of hats for them," Bredon told me. "His family takes it for granted that he will fix anything that goes wrong." My brother gave me a sour smile. "That's what financial geniuses are supposed to do. But this time, they were pretty shaken by how close they came to losing a major fortune." Bredon looked full at me. "He wants to withdraw completely from our deal, and if he leaves, a good part of the partnership will collapse, I know it. I have to find new partners, or it will be the end for me."

My heart felt like a lump of ice, frozen by fear, aching for my brother's quiet suffering over making such a wrong call. "There's my money, Bredon..."

"Never!" He did not raise his voice. He did not have to. There was no compromise on this, I could see by his eyes, by the set of his face.

"Bredon, we're family, we have only each other, whatever I have is yours too, please..."

"No, Dray, I won't do that. I have until next Monday to finalize everything. I may still be able to pull it out. I have a lot of work to do, contacting people and trying to re-work this deal. But whatever happens, the money our parents left to you is for *you*, for your future, for your life."

"*You* are my future and my life, Bredon. I don't think I could have gone on..." I stopped, having to control myself, to look calm. But my brother's urgency and sadness and peril made me want to cry, to hug him. My struggle for control had to be obvious to him.

Bredon's eyes softened. "There's still an outside chance, Dray. I haven't given up. Don't worry until you have to." He smiled. "Don't worry even then."

"How could Rand just back out like that," I said bitterly, feeling all my love and desire for him suffocated by my anxiety over my brother.

"That's why we've been arguing," Bredon said with a matching bitterness. Then he gave me an intense look. "But you spent time with him that day you met him."

Of course Bredon knew what had happened. Information is

the coin of the realm among people like Bredon, to prevent being blindsided by opponents, by financial enemies, by competing bidders. Financial success depends on many kinds of informants, as well as a good reading of markets, and strong nerves when there are big risks. I wondered how much he knew.

"I went to the Balthus show with Rand, and then we went to dinner," I told my brother, who nodded, pretending to be not-too-interested, pretending to eat, as I was pretending to eat.

"He got a phone call, and sent me home in his car," I continued.

My brother nodded, and I realized that Marilisa had told him everything she had seen.

"I was a bit mussed up," I said with pretend primness, "but I was home by midnight." Finally I had got a smile from my brother.

"He sent me roses," I added, since he already knew that too.

Bredon seemed to concentrate on his meal, not looking at me. I think he was considering asking me if I intended to see Rand again. How could I? I would be going out with a man who had caused my brother such grief. I knew that Bredon was torn, as I was. He did not want to interfere with my happiness, yet it must have been difficult for him to think of me with Rand. I was not going to cause my brother more suffering. We had had too much of that.

"I won't be seeing him any more anyway," I said, using a careless tone. "I still haven't got myself organized now that the semester is over, and then I wanted to vacation with Robin." I sipped my wine and tried to look empty-headed and indifferent. "If Robin's family is okay, I want us to go exploring Paris. Just for a couple of weeks." I shook my napkin over my lap for no reason, just to have somewhere to look as I invented these plans. In reality, trekking around a foreign city *was* the kind of thing I had done in the past, going off with a friend, growing familiar with a new place. It was an escape for me after our parents died, and I had explored Rome with a high school classmate and her mother, and the next vacation time the three of us had gone to Florence for two weeks.

Bredon studied me, probably wondering if I was being truthful. But one thing I can always do is act. My mother loved it when I would pretend to be someone else, making her laugh with my airs and my imitations of other people. My father would just look perplexed. Where did this daughter come from?

I looked at Bredon with a warm, steady smile, not a care in the world, happy just to be here, at this moment. It worked. To my great relief. I hardly knew what I had eaten, having pushed most of it around on my plate. Generally a high-end restaurant chef will take offense at such behavior, but Bredon was golden, and if this pair of Cooper children had not eaten a meal, not even half a Gallic eyebrow would be raised. My brother's generosity, and quiet separate gratuities to the youngest and poorest of the staff, the immigrant boys sending money home to their families, had them adoring him. Bredon's special feeling for these young men, alone in a new world, resonated to our own orphaned status, a world without mother and father. I loved my brother's compassion. It was also the reason he suffered so much at loss and betrayal. It was the reason for the steeliness of his exterior, to conceal a tenderness his competitors would gladly have used. To the world, Bredon seemed armored against all hurt, able to taken on any challenge, and in the world of high finance this was key for success.

"Do you want to come to my place for some coffee?" I asked Bredon.

"No, Dray, thanks, but I'm kind of wiped. I need to get some sleep before I start phoning Indonesia." He grinned. "I figure a couple of hours' sleep, and then I'll make my first calls."

"I'm going to be praying very hard," I said. I meant it.

"I appreciate that, kiddo. I hope heaven is listening." He grinned again, but this time there was the sadness over two people in heaven who would for sure be listening. I just hoped our parents were not sad for us, though I did not see how they could *not* be sad while we were all apart like this. I missed my parents so much, and I believed in my heart that they missed us too.

As we left the restaurant, murmurs of "Good-night, Monsieur Cooper, Mademoiselle," accompanied us out the door of the restaurant and into the waiting car. We were at my building within ten minutes. I kissed my brother several times, punctuating his cheeks with "good-night," "I love you, Bredon," and his "Love you too, Baby Sister" and a parting smile.

Once in my apartment I switched on the "do not disturb" switch, a little orange light that sat under a small flap by the front door where only Marilisa knew to look. I wanted to cry, to scream, feeling pain for Bredon, feeling my head pounding in fear for my brother, and a loss of what I thought would have been the most fantastic love.

My needs had to be put aside now. Rand could no longer be my preoccupation. I had thoughts to think, plans to make, to help Bredon despite his determined refusal of my help. Outwardly, the best I could do for him was to love him and be present for him. But I could also make secret plans, to help him financially. I was determined, however I could manage it, whatever it required, that I was not going to let my brother go under.

Bredon knew all the significant people in the financial world. But he did not know all of them personally, and there were still, thankfully, many ethical financiers. Among the best of these were the parents of my friend and classmate Dina. Her parents were financial wizards in their own right, an investment team, and they could be trusted to keep the confidences that financial advisors were supposed to keep. I knew instinctively that I could plan with them to hide investments in Bredon's venture under dummy names.

I thought of them because of the way we had met. By the time our college winter break had started this past December, Dina had been cut off by her friends. She had been part of a fashion-conscious, status conscious clique; had we been in high school, her group would be called "the mean girls." After their break with her, they treated Dina as a pariah, and it was all because of a boy whom I thought was worthless and horrid. He had been the boyfriend of that group's "leader," a viper of a girl who probably found him to be her perfect mate. My parents had known that boy's family, and I remembered how my parents had exchanged glances of distaste when they were mentioned in a conversation.

The semester had officially ended the day before, giving us a free ten days before Christmas. We would not return to school until late in January. Women of the various class years were milling about in front of the main hall of the College and spilling through the iron gates, all of us leaving for the long holidays. Dina stood there in despair as her friends said their good-byes to each other, walking past her and looking the other way, going to their waiting families, friends, cars, taxis. Her frantic sense of loss and abandonment struck a too-familiar chord in me, and I went to stand next to her.

She was surprised but grateful to have one classmate beside her, even though we had not really been friends during the semester. The women in her group socialized only with each other. Being close friends with someone outside their group was seen as contemptible betrayal. I found their attitudes and exclusivity appalling, and undoubtedly they regarded me and Robin as hopeless and beyond help. Even though Bredon considered one of the most "eligible" men in the city, I was dismissed by them, I think, as an aberration, yet another unfortunate relative in an important family. They seemed oblivious to the known bond I shared with Bredon, and they certainly thought me odd to spend so much time with Robin. These "mean girls" were certainly bright academically, but they were impossible snobs and narcissists. And just as they had demanded total commitment and involvement while Dina was one of their group, they were equally ruthless in ignoring her after she fell for that terrible boy. And so, at the term's end and amid the many holiday good-byes, there she stood as the crowd slowly thinned, trying not to look at the women whom she thought would be her lifelong friends.

A couple of women from that circle were still waiting to leave when Bredon's car pulled up at the college gates and he came rushing to find me, all camel-colored cashmere coat and white silk scarf, looking tall and wonderful, causing the murmurs that usually occurred when he appeared. He embraced me happily, a quick kiss on the cheek, making me feel so reassured and safe. I put my hand on Dina's arm.

"Bredon, this is my friend Dina," I told him, to her grateful surprise.

"Merry Christmas, Dina," Bredon said, bending to kiss her lightly on the cheek. "Have a good holiday."

"You too..." and she was afraid to call him by his first name, which made me smile at her, and I saw her parents coming up behind her. She saw my look and turned to see them, so happy and relieved as they put their arms around her, smiling at us, her father giving her a peck on the cheek.

"Mother, Daddy, this is Dray Cooper, and her brother Bredon. My parents..." she began, but Bredon stopped her with a smile, saying, "I recognized you, Mr. and Mrs. Ayers," and they quickly said together, "Rae and Bobby." They had not either needed an introduction to my brother.

"So nice meeting you," Bredon said, none of us shaking hands because arms were wrapped around each other, I and Bredon, Dina and her parents. We began moving toward Bredon's car.

"'Bye," Dina said to me, her eyes saying thank-you as she also began moving off, her parents each holding one of her arms, their car probably further up Broadway, cars double-parked and illegally parked everywhere, waiting for their passengers.

I could see that Dina's former friends were showing new interest in her, Bredon's appearance having accomplished that magic. But Dina held her ground, looking at none of them. I was cheering her on, and was only sorry that Robin had left so much earlier. She would have enjoyed helping Dina stand against the group she called "The Medusa Collective."

When we returned to school for the spring semester, Dina had decided to begin the pre-med program, a heavy schedule of demanding science courses. Still, in her rare free time she would meet with Robin and me for a quick lunch, or for one of the special events that the University had almost every weekend. She never mentioned the December day when we had become friends, and I only told Robin that Bredon and I had met Dina's parents. Robin could see the whole picture, for it was obvious to everyone that Dina no longer had any use for the women who, just last semester, had been her best friends.

With a whispered prayer of gratitude to heaven that I now knew the Ayers, I made my plan. If Bredon could not pull it off, or find other partners, or get Rand to change his mind, I would go to the Ayers' financial group, RRA (Rae and Robert Ayers Investment Group, the simplest acronym as Dina smilingly had told me) and hope they could help me. They were people who had the gift of gratitude, and I knew Dina well enough now to know that she had told her parents the whole story of that day in December.

I had been pacing around my apartment as I thought about all of this, and I noticed the text message light was on again. "Tomorrow, Darling. Late afternoon? R." I felt the rush of sexuality and heat just seeing his initial, and felt the irony of it all. Did Rand really think nothing had changed? That he could back out on Bredon but go on with me?

I knew I had to be careful about showing anger toward Rand. He might still come through for Bredon. Well, I would put him off until all final decisions were made. At least, I hoped that I could do that. Robin's words came back to me, and I did not want to make God laugh by planning all our futures.

It was late now. I had been pacing, barefoot, thinking, praying for a couple of hours and was too wired to sleep. I had pulled off my outside clothes, and was wearing the light at-home loose tunic and pants that doubled as loungers or pajamas. I went into my medicine chest and got a couple of nighttime aspirin, downed them with a huge glass of water, and fell into bed assuming I would just lie awake, but my exhaustion took hold, and I dropped into a sleep filled with Gothic scenes of danger, flashes of faces from the past and the present, a Freudian textbook for any therapist.

VI

It was coming on to the Summer Solstice, June twenty-first, and the nights were getting ever shorter. I had not pulled up the blackout screen on my shades, so the early dawn woke me, still tired from the emotions of last evening and the dream-filled night. My first waking thoughts were of Bredon. Sitting up in my bed I dialed him, only then realizing that such an early call might make him worry about *me*. Sure enough, his voice was anxious, so I quickly assumed a cheerful tone, as though neither of us were at a precipice in our lives.

"I *know* you're at the office," I trilled. "You are, aren't you? Just calling to check on whether you stayed awake." My tone was light, but I was holding the phone with a death grip.

"Yes, I'm awake." He gave a low laugh, brief, a tiny interlude in his long hours already spent on the phone.

"Any chance that you'll get *some* kind of nap today?" My tone remained light, but I wanted to shoo the world from his office, push him onto one of his sofas, cover him with a blanket, and let him sleep. He had done that so often for me when I was a little girl, falling asleep on a sofa in our parents' house, especially during the long summer afternoons after I had been swimming and running and swimming some more. Oh, Bredon, I thought, how I wish we were all together now, back there, the four of us. I bit my lower lip, taking deep breaths, which he heard.

"Did *you* sleep?" he challenged me.

"Of course I did. I just wanted to call you, even before I've had coffee."

"Ah, so even you can be sleepy in the morning," he said, teasing me because I usually came awake so totally, the minute my eyes opened.

"What happened with your overnight calls?" I asked, praying that he had had good news.

"The Indonesian group is interested," he said, his voice stronger. "And I had a long call with a Chinese group. They've promised to meet today on my proposal." I said another silent prayer of thanks and supplication, imploring heaven to let everyone say yes to Bredon's plan.

My brother hesitated just a beat. "That leaves Rand. He's coming in from India this morning. I'm going to give it another go, and try to convince him to opt in." Another almost imperceptible hesitation. "He probably only said yes to meeting me because of you."

"Then I'm glad we went out," I said with hard-voiced loyalty, making my brother chuckle. "When will he be there?"

"He's coming here straight from the airport. No sacrifice, since he's coming in by private jet." My brother's low laugh was sarcastic and bitter and sad. I felt my stomach knot. I realized that Bredon thought I wanted to continue seeing Rand. Unthinkable.

To make my feelings clear to Bredon without mentioning Rand, I used my bossy younger sister voice and said, "When you're done, call me, okay? Let's meet for a late lunch. And then you can sleep!" I never mentioned Rand, as though his time with Bredon was simply an inconvenience in my schedule.

Bredon made an "ooh, I'm sorry" sound, and said, "Dray, I can't. Sorry, kiddo. I told Rand that we would have a luncheon meeting, because his plane will arrive about eleven and he'll be in the city around lunch time. But I'll call you after, okay? We'll have dinner…"

"No, Bro," I said teasingly, and I should have won an Oscar just for this morning's acting. "After you have your meeting with him, please, please, go home and sleep!"

"Okay, okay," he said comically, getting into the spirit of my teasing. Then that brief hesitation again. He did not want to interfere if I wanted to see Rand. I knew it, felt it.

"If you wake up by seven tonight, call me and we'll have a quick dinner," I said. "Otherwise, just call me when your meeting is over, and tell me how it went, and we'll have breakfast tomorrow. Okay?" I hoped that my cheery plans answered his unspoken question about my seeing Rand. But Bredon knew Rand.

"He's going to want to see you, Dray, no matter what. It was pretty clear that he was taken with you." Bredon's voice was gentle, a statement. His tone contained no questions and no judgment. But the tone of my answer was drawling sarcasm.

"Yes, well, I'm busy, and maybe my schedule will open up sometime later in the year." I yawned with no effort, truly tired from the past night, making my brother laugh the way we did when we were all alive and together and enjoying the give-and-take of teasing. I remembered our parents' delight when Bredon and I had these conversations, and my heart scrunched itself up as I pictured those scenes, their clarity in my mind so sharp, so lovely and so painful. Remembering in this way always made the world feel so empty. For all my "recovery" from the tragedy, my hold on life was an indifferent one. I held on for Bredon's sake, and I knew there were times that he had only held on for me. I did not want him to wonder at my silence, so I yawned again, a bit noisily, and "oh, sorry, yawn, yawn."

"Okay, kiddo, talk to you later," Bredon said, his voice a bit lighter.

"Maybe you can nap before he gets to your office," I suggested.

"Dangerous. I might be too groggy to function," he said, all business. But I had put an idea into his head, because he added, "I'll tell Mrs. Andrews to check on me by ten thirty. And it sounds like you can use some more sleep."

He had been awake all night and he wanted *me* to sleep. I prayed that my brother would have wild amounts of adrenalin to overcome his own fatigue. I resented that Rand would arrive well-rested, no long security or passport lines for him, his clearance arranged in advance. The private international charter and corporate jets had luxury full-length beds. Rand would have slept during the final leg of his trip, waking as though he had spent the night at home. Probably, his plane was a family holding, like the building he lived in, and heaven only knew what else.

That day when Robin visited me, before we had to say good-bye again, she whispered like a conspirator that she planned to do all sorts of internet searches on him, and seek out all the gossip about him that she possibly could. I ignored the gossip circuit, and I could not care less about what Rand's family owned. Right now I only hated the thought that my brother might be exhausted at this critical meeting, and his traitorous deserter of a partner would be full of energy.

Well, I would *will* energy into my brother's spirit, I would be the witch that men suspected resided in every woman's soul. And the saint. I would pray like mad to every saint; Saint Teresa, who withstood all kinds of illness and maintained her sense of humor, her irony, her mystical arc to heaven, reforming the Carmelites in the process. Balance, sanity, tolerance, wondrous love, a perfect saint to intercede for Bredon. And I would ask Saint Anthony, the miracle finder, that Bredon find all the money he needed, and Saint Jude, the patron saint of hopeless causes, to add his intercession just in case Bredon's deal was teetering toward disaster. And of course, God, the Great Spirit, Jesus, The Holy Spirit, The Virgin, all the Angels, St. Michael especially, that super Archangel, Bredon's favorite celestial being. We were Anglicans, very high-church, and one of my classmates, a Methodist, had once said, "You people are no better than the Roman Catholics." That had sent me into gasping laughter, because Methodists also call themselves Catholics, right in their prayer book, which the girl obviously did not know. And I was laughing because Robin was sputtering in protest, offended on my behalf, saying, "How dare you be so narrow-minded?" Robin, whose family was Jewish, loved my stories about the holy people of the world, including that Saint Teresa's family was Jewish. The double irony, of the saint's character and her background, perfectly suited Robin's comically wry view of the world.

Morning coffee had not compensated for the night I'd had, and I was tired, unusually so. Generally I was full of energy in the morning hours, but as I read The Times, the sunlight coming onto the window seat of my study alcove warmed me, then lulled me into sleepiness. Thinking I would lie down for a few minutes, since I was still in my bed-and-lounge clothes, I felt the emotional fatigue and the sleep-troubled night overtake me. The world faded to dreams.

It was almost four when I woke up. I had kept all the phones on, and ran to check my cell phone – no message – and then my little back-up cell phone that folded so thinly, took pictures, had a few apps, but best for its phone and its smallness. It was the one I most traveled with, the phone Bredon often called first. No message. Before I could reach it, the heart-attack ring of my land line sounded, a shrill sound I kept meaning to get changed but which served well as a literal wake-up call.

An unnecessary glance at caller ID. "Hello, Bredon."

"Hi, Dray." His voice had a studied calm. Things had not gone well.

"What did Rand say?" I was trying not to sound as overwrought as I felt.

"His family was so spooked by the near failure in India, they're insisting on closing down all investments like our deal, at least for a while. Rand told me that he still was open to the possibilities, but the family's pressure was pretty intense."

"So can everything just be put on hold while you do other projects?" I was frantically praying he would say yes, and my stomach curled as he said, "No, not possible. I am going to be flying out later tonight. Kuala Lumpur will be my first stop. You'll have my full itinerary from Mrs. Andrews, and yes, I'll sleep on the flight." I could sense his sad grin. "I should be back by Sunday night."

We were not spooked by flying. Bredon and I took jets after our parents' deaths, and for some reason I never feared that we too would be blown out of the sky. Perhaps I simply did not care. If our parents' deaths do anything at all, they prepare us for our own mortality. And the danger now was more on the ground than in the air, armies everywhere. Then I thought, well, Kuala Lumpur is not Paris, but no place was truly safe anymore.

These thoughts had gone quickly through my mind. "Can I come?" I asked.

"No, for obvious reasons and reasons that make me too angry to discuss."

I knew he meant that when men who brought women who were not their wives, it was assumed that the women would be bribes and bonuses. They would sleep with the other men in exchange for a smoother deal. In effect, it was a pimping process, a woman in exchange for money. Bredon had always refused to do that. I wondered if Rand had also always refused. But in any case, no, I would not be going on this trip, nor would Bredon's girlfriend Ree, whose real name was Ariana Cleves. Like so many of us, she'd had a couple of names conferred on her at her baptism, babies among the rich often named for the maternal line. My mother, for example, was a Drayman. And Bredon was the family name of my father's mother.

Bredon and Ariana were very private and discreet, often spending weekends at our family lodge far upstate in New York, going by separate small planes out of Teterboro Airport, flying to the little county airport down the road from our lodge. A married couple lived in the caretaker's cottage on the grounds there. They cleaned and tended the house and land, hiring additional help as needed, to cut trees or do major skilled electrical work or carpentry. Usually, the husband would pick up Bredon and then go back for Ree when her plane landed. The lodge was owned under a corporate name completely different from any of the family's publicly known holdings, so it was a true retreat, but far away and requiring time, weather, and flight coordination. With their marriage on hold since our parents' death, the lodge was their hideaway where they could spend long hours together without public notice or fuss.

Ree was lovely, her character gentle, far gentler than mine. There was no way that Bredon would expose her, beautiful and kind person that she was, to the open leers that she would be sure to receive from the international financial dealers. Supposedly worldly, they retained their narrow moralism, convinced that all Americans are sexually free, which made all American women potential prostitutes. I had no desire to see and be ogled by such men, but I did not want Bredon to feel even more alone than he must have felt now, with this deal so tenuous.

"Can I at least drive with you to the airport? Have coffee with you?"

"I'm keeping this trip very quiet, Dray," and he did not have to explain why. No rumors should even be whispered, even speculatively, about the unusual enormity of the risk Bredon was taking. He wanted no word anywhere that there might be a problem.

I decided a light approach was needed to counterbalance the hard realities that had us so sober and thoughtful. "All right, Big Bro, do your thing, go and make deals. Knock 'em dead." I grinned, for I had used the words he would use when I was a little girl about to appear in a school play or was starting a tennis game.

When we hung up I realized how hungry I was, and how much I had neglected everything, mail, messages, reading, friends. My occasional disappearances from view were thought to be caused by lapses into depression. The assumption that I retreated to grieve was occasionally true, and also served to keep people from asking questions about where I was. On rare occasions Bredon and I would spend time with a couple of cousins, to gather "family" time in some form. Mostly, I roamed the city's endlessly changing neighborhoods, the clusters of ethnicities making little cities in the big one. I visited museums, I visited churches. My alone times were to renew myself, and Bredon could always reach me by the little phone whose number only he possessed. My calls from that phone came up as "restricted number," another of Bredon's privacy tactics.

Preoccupied with thoughts of Bredon, not wanting to talk to any friends because I was so restless over him, I decided to order a meal from a nearby Turkish restaurant, a new, upscale place that quietly packaged and sent out prepared meals to people in our vicinity. Many people did not want to go to a restaurant at the end of a long day, nor to cook, nor order from a place that did only takeout. And I wanted to go to church, I wanted to attend evening prayer services at St. Mary's if they had one tonight, and whether or not there was a service, to light candles, and pray, and think. But first I called Marilisa.

"Please," I said, "come take the roses. Their scent is gorgeous, but now I'm getting a headache from them!"

Of course she knew better. "I'll come for them now. Do you mind if I keep them in my apartment?"

"Yes, keep them," I said, play-acting cheerful indifference, not fooling her one bit. Neither of us wanted to waste the beauty of those flowers.

She was there and gone, with the roses, within ten minutes.

As I was about to call the restaurant on my land line, the phone rang with a caller ID number and no name. It was the local 212 area code, and I wondered if it were a friend whose name was not in my phone's directory. Generally, I wait for the message to begin, and I have told everyone, "If you don't talk to my machine, you don't talk to me." Anyone who had any of my phone numbers knew this. Robo-calls hung up when the machine came on. I resented phone calls most of the time, intrusions, unless I had planned a call with a friend. Which is why I turned my ringers off most of the time. But I had forgotten that all ringers on all phones were operating because I had been waiting for Bredon's call.

The message recording started: "Dray, this is Rand." And he waited. When I did not pick up he said, "Dray, please, I want to see you. Please pick up."

It made my heart pound to hear him, and the chemistry of him affected me, but I also resented his backing out on Bredon, I didn't care *what* pressure his family put on him.

"Dray," he said again, "please pick up. Just for a moment."

I picked up the receiver and held it to my ear. My body was warm, excited all on its own by his voice. I waited silently.

"Dray, can I see you?"

My mouth was dry. I said, "I can't."

"Because of Bredon."

"Rand, the old saying not to mix business with pleasure, seems to be good advice. I can't see you."

"But you'd see me if I'd said yes to Bredon and the deal." His voice was hard and sad.

"Rand, the situation is impossible. Please don't ask. Monday night was wonderful. That's why I picked up the phone at all. But I can't…"

He cut me off. "Just see me. For a little while. You know you're attracted to me. You know I find you wildly exciting. I love what we had on Monday."

"Yes, it was wonderful, but I can't, it's not something I can do, Rand, I'm sorry." But I wasn't sorry. It was a lie. I make no apologies for putting my brother first. Still, Bredon said Rand promised to reconsider. I wondered. "Rand, I'm going to hang up now."

"I'll call you later," he said, his voice dispirited and angry and sad, all those.

I was upset and restless, because the chemistry of his voice still affected me, and I pulled on nondescript "college student" clothes, jeans, t-shirt, light hoodie, walking shoes over white socks. I stuck my little phone in one pocket, and my flat wallet with its neatly slotted credit cards, cash, ID, and special house key, in another jeans pocket. I pulled a fragrant handkerchief from a small drawer. It had been a major joke among my friends, as it had been among my mother's friends, that we used these rather than tissues. Only when I had a cold did I forgo them.

I quickly tied my hair back, put on a baseball cap and dark glasses and slipped out the back entrance. I had a feeling that Rand would come here and try to see me. He had enough clout and power to get past most of the barriers in the lobby. Avoiding the possibility I exited through a service door to a short alley, onto the side street, and began making quick strides in the city rush hour, walking downtown at a brisk pace toward the Times Square area and St. Mary's. As I blended into the crowds on the sidewalks and at the crosswalks, I looked so ordinary, like any other girl. It was wonderful to breathe easy, to be anonymous.

The long walk calmed me, the passing crowds distracting my mind so that I had to concentrate on navigating among the flow of people. In the theatre district I walked past the oddly assorted souvenir shops, taverns, garages, side-street boutique hotels to the mid-street where St. Mary's stood, the flag high on a flagpole in front. I ran up the few steps and through the main doors. Inside, all was peace and beauty. The organist must have been rehearsing for a concert or a sung Mass, along with a couple of choristers who were singing different lines in Latin. The effect was soothing, the world continuing, the business of worship being perfected.

I moved quickly and with little footfall along the northern aisle of the church, its beauty as always inviting yet another discovery of its art, statuary, symbols, all candlelight and low electric lights, statues in their side-altars, marriage chapel, baptistry, to the Lady Chapel, my favorite. There I lighted some candles, symbols of things religious and holy, the light of Presence, and pulled neatly folded flat bills from my wallet to stuff in the offering box. I sat and thought of Bredon, saying a prayer for his safe arrival and successful bargaining, remembering our parents, letting my mind empty of everything but the feeling of being in a holy place. I stayed an hour, my mind clearing, calmer. I realized that I was very, very hungry. The evening prayer service was short, and when it was over I began my return walk, cautious whenever I saw one of the many black cars that carried Rand and so many of the people we knew as they came here for plays and restaurants.

I stopped at a small convenience store that only stayed open this late because with summer, the many tourists made late hours worthwhile. Most delis and small food stores in commercial areas of the city specialized only in breakfast and lunch on weekdays, and did not open on weekends since there were no workers to patronize the stores. The mid-town area with theatres and hotels was different. Tourists might buy snacks, and hotel guests would stock up on munchies and snacks for their rooms. Many deli patrons were hotel guests wanting something light to eat that did not have the high hotel price tags attached. The counterman made up a sandwich for me, the inimitable New York hard roll holding thinly sliced cheeses and meats, lettuce for crunch, all wrapped in an envelope of heavy waxed paper. I took a can of seltzer from the refrigerator case and ate while I walked along Central Park West, sipping the seltzer through a straw poked into the tab hole. It felt wonderful to be eating and drinking at last.

My walking meal finished, I hailed a cab, carrying the food wrappers and soda can with me for recycling. I had the cab stop a block away from my building, and let myself in the back way, a quick wave to one of the janitors who thought all young people were sneaky-crazy but harmless, and so he ignored me.

The message light blinked on my phone. I knew the number

now. "Please, Dray, please meet me. Tonight if you can, or tomorrow. I miss you. Please let's talk." Rand's voice was courting me, yet angry. It was one thing to negotiate in a business deal, but I was sure he was used to getting the women he wanted. Rich men become more "beautiful," the richer they get. If after Monday Rand felt ill-used, well, so did I, on Bredon's behalf. The phone rang as I finished hearing the message. It was Rand again. I picked up, saying nothing.

"Dray, please say something."

"Rand, hello. I just got back in. And I'm very tired," and realized as I said it that it was true, despite all the sleep I'd had today. I think my anxiety over Bredon was draining my energy, and I had prayed so intensely for him in church, I had felt light-headed between emotion and hunger when I was done.

Amazingly, he understood. "You're a sleepyhead, or so I've been told," he said in a new voice. "So, get some rest. But I've been thinking about why you won't see me. I have a thought that may change your mind." And now Rand's voice grew hard. "I want to talk to you about the deal with Bredon. Please see me."

"Rand, if word goes out that you've pulled out of the deal with Bredon, and then people see us together, I'd be – and feel like – the world's biggest traitor. I won't do that."

His voice was harder now. "Interestingly, I actually understand how you feel," he said, a stripe of anger and irony in his voice. "That's why I want to see you. I have some thoughts about the deal. And us."

"I'm seeing someone else," I lied.

"Really." A sarcastic slash of a word, six letters like a knife. "Listen," he said, "I just want to talk to you. Just meet with me, just once."

My silence was thick with my reluctance and conflict. I was wishing I could just cry or scream, I wanted him so much. But he heard only the reluctance, and I could almost feel his anger increasing. "Meet me," he insisted, his voice now like steel.

"Come to my private house. Tomorrow, two o'clock." And after a slight pause he said, tauntingly, "Your brother will benefit."

His voice had turned cruel, maybe the voice his enemies heard, and my body was in collapse over his tone, and then my own anger rising, adding to the maelstrom of my emotions. I was feeling sick to my stomach, a headache starting to take hold like a vise. His indifference to my love for my brother, using that love to get me to talk to him, to *benefit* Bredon, how dare he. He wanted to play this game with me? All right, let's see what cards he held.

"Benefit my brother," I said, repeating his words in a voice like ice. "How would that be possible, exactly?"

"In a way that I will set out in detail exactly," he answered, imitating my own arctic tone.

"Isn't there somewhere else we can meet?" I said, wary. With cameras everywhere, with the many people who knew us by sight, I did not want to be seen entering his private park or his house. Word would surely get back to Bredon, and who knew how many other people. The professional gossips had ears on the streets, and the media would snake into our lives again.

He seemed to realize my concerns but I realized that he had his own concern for privacy. If he was going to help Bredon, he was going to have to deal with his suddenly risk-averse family. "My house is the one place I can be absolutely sure we won't be overheard," he said.

My mind explored other possibilities frantically – use one of our family cars, use a hired car, rent a car, take a train to some public place where I wasn't known, but every one of those alternatives had its problems with being followed or seen or discovered. I decided to use a disguise such as Bredon and I had used to escape reporters after the air crash.

"Are you going to stand by your commitment to Bredon?" I asked, stalling.

"That's what we're going to discuss." If his voice were any

colder, I would be a cube of ice.

I gave in. "All right, two o'clock tomorrow, at your house. Your security camera won't recognize me, but it will be me. Whoever you think it is, just open the gate."

Now he was wary. "Are you going to send someone else?"

"No. It will be me."

After spending the next couple of hours fretting over Bredon and the whole crazy situation with Rand, I finally fell asleep. It was like the way I slept after our parents were killed, when the doctors had given me powerful sedatives to get me to sleep and to keep me asleep. My body had fought the drugs, which were supposed to suppress some REM sleep and dreams. Instead, more often than not, I would waken from nightmares. The doctors finally figured out a sleeping pill regimen, and a drug cocktail, that could give me about seven hours' rest. Finally. It took them a couple of weeks to get to that solution, Bredon beside himself with his own grief and worry over me. Tonight I had dreams, not nightmares, my unconscious playing out a surreal and lopsided world, absurd, skewed, cryptic, elements of Balthus puzzles in them, and the saints consoling me.

VII

Bredon wakened me on Thursday with an early call. He sounded upbeat. His first meetings had gone well, though no firm commitments were in place yet. I could not tell if he was deceiving me, or himself, or if there really was hope in these investors. But his voice was strong, and he was getting ready to go to sleep himself. He was over nine thousand miles away, and on the Equator, and I felt so lonely for him.

"What are your plans for the day?" he asked.

"I'm going to hit the museums, I think. I'm still enjoying the novelty of being on vacation from school, and Robin isn't back yet, so I'll do city exploring on my own." I often did this, no surprises, and no mention of Rand.

"What about your other friends?" he asked offhandedly, a pretended lightness.

"I may call Dina to see if she's back in Westchester. She went away with her parents right after school closed. She's probably looking for down time too." My voice was chatty, girl talk-y, avoiding seriousness. But my heart was still troubled over my brother. I sighed, quietly, and thought I heard him sigh too. We two children, each other's beacon. "Oh, Bredon, I can't wait for you to get home!"

He laughed, relieved, interpreting my sigh as missing him, which it was, and more. "Sunday night, Sis, but I'll be flying in late."

"However late, call me."

"Okay. But fair warning. The following Tuesday morning I go out again, this time for a week."

"More investors on this deal?" What was he doing, I wondered.

"No, they'll be site inspections, making sure all the offices and support staff are in place." He was positive, reassuring. But he did not say he had the money commitments he needed.

"Okay," I said, keeping my voice light. "Sunday night." I hung up and said a dozen fervent prayers for my brother, begging my parents to watch over him.

Returning to the everyday, hungry, I checked in the refrigerator; butter and eggs were there along with the heavy cream I loved in my coffee. Happily, Marilisa had left some fresh rolls on the counter, so breakfast was an easy task. I ate and thought and planned, and when I finished, I turned on the "don't come in" light, then engaged the special door locks, front and back entrances, that even Marilisa did not know about. Bredon had had these installed when no one was about on my floor, using skilled men who owed him favors. Bredon did not elaborate on who the men were, or what favors had been done. I knew not to ask.

Safely locked away from the world, I went to the back of my bedroom closet, which held yet another room behind its back wall. What had been an "owner's closet" to store things if the apartment was sublet, had been made to disappear. It just looked like a back wall now, but it was actually a pocket door, beautifully designed to be unnoticeable. Unhooking the latch, I rolled the wall to one side. There was a clothes pole at the front of the closet, a low set of drawers against one side, and boxes of shoes on the floor.

I moved aside the clothes, each outfit in its own plastic bag, and stepped over the boxes into the tiny dressing room that held a diminutive vanity table and cushioned stool. The walls held shelves with different wigs in their round shiny black boxes, and rectangular clear plastic boxes with various hats and caps. All of the clothing was from department and chain stores, ordered on line and sent to our postal drop. Bredon had a matching room hidden in his penthouse. Before he moved from his old apartment where he had also had a closet like this, he had it removed, opening up the area to make it look like a part of the deep walk-in closet, no traces of the secret storage remaining. The new tenants would never know.

We lived in a kind of paranoia, a lifestyle more like spies than normal siblings after the air crash. We did all we could to hide from the ghoulish curiosity of reporters, from brash, intrusive people we did not know, who saw themselves as well-meaning, who proffered sympathy and banalities and sometimes "religious" consolations that drove us crazy. After the bombing a torrent of newspaper reporters had clustered at the survivors' houses. For days there were programs streamed and on television, with panels of experts discussing the terrorists, the flight, the passengers, whether one or more passengers had been targeted. The newspapers, and some commentators, milked every detail for its possible shock factor. There were constant attempts to reach families of the lost passengers by phone, twitter, text when a cell number could be found.

I was in such a shaken condition that after a short hospital stay, I was sequestered in our great-aunts' house in Riverdale, while Bredon worked to keep the media craziness from reaching me. He hired his own technical wizard to block every digital attempt to access us.

Then it was a matter of not being bothered when we left home to go outside, to walk or take a car or a cab. When we appeared on the street there were "death stalkers," those perverse freaks who were fascinated with the deaths and grief of the famous. Hating their eager, vulgar attempts to engage us in conversation, we had devised our plans for disguises, inspired by our parents' friendships with several actors, and our own school plays.

We had the help of "Toro" Tomàs, now a character actor in movies and television dramas, who had been Bredon's prep school classmate. He had been bullied for his size, and declared stupid, clumsy, inferior, by the dreadful snobbish older students who seemed to lack conscience or compassion. Tomàs' parents were rich, and had sent him to the U.S. to give him the best private education possible. Unknowingly, they had consigned their son to the misery of difference and foreignness.

The heartlessness of some of the boys, raised in rich entitlement, led them to mock anyone who somehow provoked their dislike. It had enraged Bredon, who had come to Tomàs' defense. Our parents' wealth, and my brother's own tall, handsome elegance became a protective shield for his tormented friend. Tomàs had never forgotten. When Bredon had contacted him after the bombing and the assaults by the press, he found his way to us by one of the unseen entrances to our building, and spent an evening teaching us about disguises, telling us what things to buy and how to use them. He had brought some make-up with him, and made Bredon's face look like that of an old and nondescript man, showing us how to "age" or "de-beautify" ourselves. I was so grateful for his genuine concern for us, and I adored his great size and the gentleness he showed us. His gratitude and friendship for Bredon were obvious, never spoken, touching my heart forever. When he was leaving I kissed him with a peck on the cheek, having to climb on top of the sofa cushion to do so, to his delighted laughter, catching me so that I could slide down his arm back to the floor. It was the first time since the bombing that Bredon and I had actually been able to laugh, and then to hug this man, a stranger to me, but someone whom I realized would always be devoted to Bredon.

The clothing and make-up along with back doors became the way we avoided notice when we wanted to go out alone. The wigs were another matter. Those were ordered through Ren, Bredon's friend and our doctor. The wigmakers assumed Ren was filling orders on behalf of his patients who had lost their hair to cancer or other illnesses, and Ren knew how to do the measurements for the under-nettings and the wigs. The good human hair wigs were very expensive and they did their work well. Once the wig was on, it was indistinguishable from natural hair.

For Bredon there had been a variety of men's wigs. Ren had

even gone to a costume shop to purchase a bald man's mask, a fringe of "hair" around the bottom of the large bald spot, and he worked with Bredon to incorporate that into one of the wigs. For me, the wigs were short and long, blonde and black and brown and red. Two were purposely purchased for the ability to make them into "hair" that was messy and unkempt. If we looked poor, or old, or hollow-eyed, wearing shapeless clothes, people would avert their eyes from us when passing. We could travel quickly and quietly, simply walking freely, no one bothering to notice us. I did this a couple of times when I needed to roam about the city, just to cope with my own restlessness, and it gave me a rare and blessed anonymity. In the early days after the bombing, disguise became my defiant answer to the sickening curiosity, and presumption, of "sympathizers."

It had been a long time since I had used these disguises. Bredon had given up on them quickly, for his financial dealings made concealment unsuitable for a man who needed people's trust. I could more easily escape notice, and had altered my appearance many times in the year after our parents' deaths.

We had taken other steps to avoid public notice. Bredon had used his governmental connections to get each of us a false federal identity card. We were John and Mary Cole, names so obvious as to be unnoticeable. Bredon did not want to risk getting us false passports, but the cards were acceptable substitutes when identification was required. And as John Cole he set up a post office box, and opened a bank account for each of us with a debit card and checking attached. Our bank statements would come to us separately at our post office box, and we each had a key to the box. I did not know how much this would help me in the future, but it was a fortunate decision.

A message-only telephone line to which Bredon alone had access, was the contact he listed for the accounts. The social security numbers we used had belonged to our dead grandparents. As the "Coles", each of us had savings, checking and a debit card. The signature cards and applications, obtained through Bredon's own bank branch, were already signed. We had practiced old-fashioned cursive signatures, and made copies to remind ourselves of the way John and Mary Cole signed their names.

Eventually the person at the bank who had opened the account would have forgotten about it. We counted on that, and by agreement, took turns using the checking accounts only once in a great while to cash a few hundred dollars, to avoid having the bank's computers flag the accounts for inactivity. The slowly accumulating deposits made in cash were to provide for some possible future case when we needed to draw money quickly without also drawing attention to our real identities. We did all this to help us should an emergency occur, should we need money quickly to disappear from public view, to be left alone to lead our lives in privacy.

For my meeting with Rand today, I would resume my post-bombing practice of disguising myself to avoid recognition and attention. With surveillance cameras everywhere, it was ever more difficult to hide from view. I would need time to make myself into a street kid of no distinction, and then get to Rand's house using the subways. So I began early, first using a hand towel to remove the small dust that had accumulated in the closet. I just gave everything a quick swipe, including the vanity table, and began.

I wound my long hair around my head, the wig cap snugly fitted over it, and then selected a wig that was a shag-pixie combination, a poorly-done haircut, in a washed-out blonde. A baseball cap and dark glasses would conceal my face, no makeup. I put little earrings on, tiny circles that could have been piercings. I snapped on the belt of an under-the-shirt pouch that would lie flat against my stomach, and hold my credit cards, I.D. and cash, and where I would also stow my apartment key. It had thin straps if I wanted to hang it around my neck, but for this disguise, I sat it low around my waist, its bottom half tucked into my panties. It was easily covered under a long-sleeved cotton shirt that fell straight to mid-hip. I pulled on department store jeans that were just a bit too large to show my figure and that were baggy at the knees. In the larger closet were molding strips, and a small hollow area behind one of them where I hid cash. I took several bills of various denominations to fold flat into my wallet, and more bills to put in one deep side pocket of my jeans. My tiny phone, with Rand's number entered, went into the other pocket. My path downtown would be by subway, and I would buy a Metro Card using cash, to avoid any credit card record of my purchase. I pulled on white socks, and scuffed running shoes. The days were growing warmer though this year we had many unusually cool days and evenings, so I took a standard type of navy blue hoodie, zipped up but draped over my shoulders, its sleeves tied together over my chest. I had put on the plainest white cotton bra and panties. No perfume. I wondered, smiling grimly to myself, whether Rand would be repulsed my scruffy plainness.

I decided to wear the dark glasses both outside and in the subways, making me even less wholesome a figure. I re-latched the closet and paced the apartment, getting myself used to the tightness of the wig cap, walking around to get used to wearing ill-fitting clothes. The trick, I had found, was to imagine another life, to create myself as a young person of no particular standing, a city child, with origins somewhere in the five boroughs, ordinary and unremarkable.

When I slipped out the back doors of my apartment and building I already had a travel plan fixed in my mind. Taking the Number 1 train, I jumped off at 31st Street and went down the block to the St. Francis church, noted for its daily Breadline that fed so many. Downstairs in the church, at the Shrine of St. Anthony, I pushed a small offering into one of the alms boxes, and said another prayer to the Saint, that Bredon would find ethical investors and all the money he needed for his project. Back on the train, I went to 14th Street, big signs on the platform saying Union Square.

Up on the streets again I walked to an F train, and down the steps to the train that said Coney Island, taking it to East Broadway. After that, I would walk as though aimlessly, in a circuitous route that wound toward Rand's house. The sidewalks were more or less crowded, the ebb and flow of people thinning as I neared the luxury area of apartment buildings, an enclave of a neighborhood where almost no stores could be found, and the foot traffic considerably diminished as a result. This was unfortunate for my plans, so I looped around and came up the side street toward the gate. I clicked the speed number for Rand.

"I'm a few yards away. Look for my baseball cap," I said without a hello or any other words, and snapped the phone closed.

I got to the gate, the street thankfully shaded by the buildings all around. Hearing the gate click, I slipped in very quickly. I moved rapidly out of sight of the street to the shielding trees and bushes and the flat stone path to Rand's door, which clicked ajar at my approach.

I knocked anyway, a few brief raps, and Rand pulled the door open, standing there squinting at me, caught between amusement and anger, his anger clearly winning. He stood back to let me enter, still no words between us. I felt the surge of attraction as I passed by him and went unasked to sit on the sofa where we had made love an age ago, a few days ago. The room was as beautiful as last time, fresh flowers, the air clean-smelling, everything clean and polished. Whoever tended this place was a treasure. I was trying to control my reaction to Rand, my desire mixed with my own anger, distracting myself by thinking about housekeeping, all to no avail.

Rand sat on a chair in front of me, and I felt warm, my heart speeding up. I did not want to look directly at him.

"Do take off those glasses, Dray," he said in an acid tone.

Oh, God, is anything ever easy?

"And would you take off the wig?"

I wanted to scream with my conflicted sadness and embarrassment. "It's difficult to get it back on," I answered, and sat without doing anything.

Rand made a sound that was like a contemptuous snort, which felt like a blow. I felt close to tears, another surprise to me, I who had trained myself not to cry in front of anyone except Bredon, and only when we were sharing hours and memories. I sat there in too much misery to say anything.

With a look of impatience, resettling himself into his chair, Rand said, "I am willing to bail your brother out."

"He doesn't need 'bailing out'," I almost hissed. "From what I understand, he just needs you to keep your word in the capital agreement."

"In other words, keep my part of the bargain – even if it's a bad bargain."

"I'm not crazy about the other partners either," I said, "but once the project is launched, lots of others will be there to jump in and buy up your shares, and Bredon's, and you'll both be out. Even if you don't make a profit – though I'm sure you will – you'll break even."

He was taken aback. I don't think he realized that I knew anything about that rather vicious financial world in which they operated, and his eyes showed their grudging respect for what I had said.

"It's still a major risk," he said.

"Yes."

"Are you willing to make a bargain with *me* to go ahead with investing in this deal?"

"In other words, a bargain so that you keep *your* bargain," I retorted.

"Bredon knew that I hadn't made a final commitment. We

agreed that I could opt out if I didn't want to continue. He just assumed that I would go ahead, that his golden touch would work this time too. But this one is very tricky, Dray. It's a major risk for me too."

His family was so rich, I doubted that he was telling the truth. But then I thought of the emergency that had torn us apart that first night. "Did you manage to pull that last set of irons out of the fire?" I asked.

Again, his surprise that I knew what had summoned him on Monday night.

"Yes. Everything is okay now." He got up and went over to the fireplace, looking at the pieces on the mantle. "So that leaves *our* bargain, the one I'll make with you, and that will give Bredon all the money he needs."

"And that is?"

"You. Are you willing to sell yourself to me to save your brother?"

"Sell myself!"

"In a sense. I want five nights with you, five Friday nights into Saturday morning. My terms are simple: sex and other things, any way I want. And from you, total compliance, and total silence. From sundown to right before sunup each time."

"So, a whore. Bought with money that will close the deal with Bredon."

"Yes, a whore." He looked at me so coldly I felt my stomach knot.

"No."

"Then he's done. His whole financial empire collapses."

I had other thoughts in my mind, but I did not correct him. I just looked at him. And I saw that he still wanted me, that the lovemaking we had done still had power over both of us. I thought, well, I want him anyway. I can take a man's point of view: sex just for sex, sex that doesn't mean anything. So I said, "I *will* bargain with you, but not on those terms."

"The bargain is your body for money."

"Yes."

"So you *would* do this for him," Rand said, almost contemptuously. "You really love the guy. It sounds a bit unnatural." He said it with the hardest, coldest tone of voice, making me more furious. How dare he, this arrogant bastard, and how could I have had such tenderness for him? My eyes must have been on fire, but I looked down, hiding my anger, deciding to match the cold and cutting knife his question was. He did not know this part of me. I could be as stony and unforgiving as he. I felt like Antigone who screamed at the man she loved, that her parents were dead, and could not give her another brother. But rather than answering him angrily, I looked at him with a bored expression.

"You have older sisters, Rand. Did they use you as a sex toy? Is that why you are thinking such disgusting things about me and Bredon?" My comment startled and infuriated him, his color rising as he began to lift himself from his chair. I think he wanted to slap me.

Then he stopped, shocked into stillness, realizing the affront he had thrown at me, and that this was the road to hatred. Something in him must have warned him off, although he was furious over my remark.

"I shouldn't have said that, Dray, I'm sorry." His voice was shaky with a mixture of coldness and true apology. I just nodded and turned my head away from him, willing my own pounding anger to subside, and my heart to calm. Between desire and fury, I felt hot, I wanted to lash out, to scream, but I clamped my emotions down, and waited.

I thought he would walk away, thinking, "Oh, well, I thought I'd give it a try." Instead he said, "What would *your* terms be? Mind you, they would have to include the sexual part." He shifted in his chair and gave me a cool stare. "Except for one thing. For some reason, unlike most men, I find the thought of a man's penis in a woman's mouth too disgusting for words. However, nothing else is off the table."

I was relieved more than I could believe. Stories of oral sex were like stories of last night's television dramas among many of my college classmates, their boyfriends demanding and pleading for fellatio, and when positions were literally reversed, how inadequate the men often were in using their tongues to pleasure the women.

"It doesn't mean that I don't get to taste you," he said slyly, cynically.

That didn't bother me. Go for it, I thought. At least I would be spared some of the more nauseating accounts of boyfriends who insisted on trying, at least, to come in their girlfriends' mouths.

"Okay, I'll make a bargain with you," I said, coolly, as though I were not feeling dirtied, yet fascinated with the thought of having him, of sex with him, because being this close to him caused a heat in me that was like the ultimate sexual itch. My desire for him still had me stunned with its power. Fleetingly I wondered again at the strange suddenness of Monday's ardor. Outwardly, I looked indifferent.

"You want no talking. I'll agree to that," I told him calmly. Play-acting.

"No sound," he corrected. "No moan or groan or anything. Silence." His eyes were cold, but amused. I wanted to smack him. I wanted to resume our interrupted night.

"No sound." I nodded, my expression conveying that I found the condition tedious. "Agreed. But *one* night, not five." He shook his head no, vigorously, no, no, no.

"Two nights, then," I countered. "But that's it." And that really was my limit. I suspected he had many kinds of sex games in mind, and was not so stupid as to think it was going to be a time of valentine sweetness.

"Two nights." He nodded. "Agreed."

Ah, I thought, that's what he intended anyway.

"And you have to wear, and do, what I say, or what I tell you I want for each night," he repeated in a cautioning tone.

"Such as?"

"No bra, no panties, no stockings. I'll let you know what else. The second time too, you wear what I tell you to wear. And in between, some other things I may tell you to do before we meet for the second time." He recited this in a hard voice. He had thought about it, I could hear. No hesitation, just condition after condition. I wondered what experiences he had had with other women, how "creative" his sexual encounters had been.

Whatever, I thought.

Now it was my turn.

"I'm making one unbreakable condition," I said. "Bredon must never know. Not ever. I swear, I will find a way to kill you if he ever finds out."

I said it very quietly and calmly, but although his eyes grew wide with shock and amusement, he simply said, "I believe you. I agree."

"Your word?"

"My word." He looked at me. "You put such store by that, by your word, and by mine?"

"Yes. It's absolute. My word is my word. I assume the same about you."

"Agreed," he nodded, very serious now. Then he added, "And in case you don't know what this bargain entails, some of it may be painful."

"I had assumed that," I lied, praying that whatever he had in mind, he would not be carried away with making me suffer. I was also wondering whether he had been careful, having read so much about herpes and AIDS and STDs. Was I letting myself in for a lifetime of payback with controllable, but incurable diseases?

"I assume this will be safe sex," I said, again pretending indifference. I had finished my period right before we had made love

89

on Monday. I did not want to become pregnant, but there was not time to get fitted for a diaphragm or get an IUD, and it took time for birth control patches or pills to work. Maybe the end of my period was tied to my lust. Nature is no fool, and desire rises when all is most ripe for pregnancy.

He was watching me. He knew he had me on this one. "Oh, no," he said, "not if you mean using condoms. No, this sex will be raw." His tone was both cruel and lustful.

Oh, God, I thought, steeling myself, continuing to pretend indifference as I nodded, as though to say, "of course, that's to be expected." In my heart I did not believe he was fooled, but I did not care. My first concern was Bredon. I would take my chances, and deal with whatever the outcomes later.

Now I had to make sure about the foundation of this whole preposterous agreement. "I have one last condition," I said, "and that's the condition for everything else." I finally looked up at him, a serious, disinterested look. "Before the banks close on Friday, at least half of the money has to be wired into Bredon's account. Once I see the confirmation, I'll come here."

"How will you see the confirmation...?" he started to ask, but then realized that my brother must have given me every necessary code to access his accounts. "You're very young to know so much about the financial world," he said, maybe disappointed that I was not living in some stupid haze of ignorance about money. "You *are* eighteen, yes?" he added, half seriously, half rhetorically. But I took his question for what it really asked.

"Yes." I smiled my own cool smile. "Eighteen. Legal."

"I want to see you tomorrow night, our first night," he said.

"Yes, okay." I nodded, cool, as though growing impatient. Time was growing short for Bredon. I would have said yes to this very night if that had been necessary. As it was, though, this brief delay gave me time. I had my own urgent preparations to make before tomorrow night.

Slipping quickly out of Rand's, I got back to a subway station and ran down the stairs onto the first train to Times Square. A fast ride and I was there, up the steps to the street, going into a large drug store, a chain with stores all over Manhattan. Making my way through the aisles to the pharmacy at the back, I pretended to be studying something next to the counter that held an extensive condom display. Hoping I would be able to use them despite Rand's refusal, I pulled a box of three condoms from the peg. There were bigger boxes, holding more than twenty, there were colors and ridges and one had feathers on the bottom, clearly shown on the front of the box. A French tickler, I thought. Randy literature had its uses. I purchased the ribbed latex ones, thinking he would at least be intrigued and try, and besides, these were the only ones in the small three-piece box. They didn't cost much more than a dollar each, though the last thing I wanted to do at that moment was comparison shop.

When the pharmacist nodded that it was my turn, I was thankful for the "privacy" panels on either side of the counter. "Plan B," I said. The "morning after" pills, to prevent pregnancy after unprotected sex.

He did not ask to see identification. Sizing me up in ten seconds, he got the pills for me. You had to be eighteen to buy the pills without a prescription, a stupid law since the sixteen-year-olds would likely be the ones who often needed it. In my Internet searches I had found the information on Plan B, and saw that coupons were offered to bring down the price from the forty or so dollars the pills cost. I was hardly going to print out the coupons, but the information on dosage and type had been useful.

I put the condoms on the counter without looking at the pharmacist and he quickly rang up the sale. The Plan B he gave me was generic but still would be expensive even for middle income people. Even so, it was far cheaper, financially and emotionally, than having a baby. I took three of the twenties in my jeans pocket, a cash sale with no record beyond the in-store cameras. I hoped my disguise and dark glasses would obscure my identity from the cameras that were everywhere now, stores and streets.

I emerged from the store amid noisy horns, rivers of people moving across the pedestrian areas in the middle of Broadway, the Times Square rush hour in its classic incarnation. It was getting cool and breezy, so I pulled the hoodie on and kept one hand in my pocket, over the small bag with the pills and condoms. No one looked at me, a city figure happily unremarkable and in fact not at all attractive. I walked northward, skirting the long-haired groups of girls and the satellite groups of worldly-wise boys orbiting around them, saying cool, flirtatious things. I was no older than they, yet I felt I had lived for a century.

At Columbus Circle I found a relatively quiet spot to phone Marilisa. "Please have a meal delivered for me," I asked her, "Turkish food if you can."

"Yes, I'll order it now. And a note was delivered for you." She said this as though this unusual event were the most ordinary thing in the world. My surprise at the note kept me silent. She did not miss a beat. "Shall I put the food and the note inside for you?" She always asked, even though the answer was always yes. Maybe she noticed how much the "do not enter" light had been on these two days.

"Yes, please, Marilisa, thank you."

"You're welcome," she said in her wonderful light voice, soft and happy. Her sweetness made me smile, lifted my spirits as I found my way back home by subway.

Once I got into the back entrance of my building I ducked into a janitor's area, a "blind spot" with no security cameras, and pulled off the wig and cap, tucking them inside my hoodie. My hair came down neatly as I unpinned it, and I looked more like myself when I got on the service elevator. Thankfully, no one else was around anyway. The janitors had gone to night shift and were elsewhere now. It felt wonderful to be home.

VIII

I could smell the aromas of the Turkish food on the dining table where Marilisa had set a place for me. I was so hungry, but first I had to see the note, which she had placed on my desk. The plain white envelope was sealed, my name in small block letter on its face. It was from Rand.

A note sent this way, probably delivered by Tom, was the perfect way to avoid electronic records and surveillance. So many figures, to their disgrace, had been publicly exposed in all meanings of the term, their texts and e-mails detailing their private lives and their naked bodies. Rand was as adept at avoiding discovery as I was. And it was all so ironic. Had he simply put in his share of money for Bredon, I would gladly have jumped into his bed, open to any sexual adventure with him. But now sex was his way of shaming me, in his anger that I chose Bredon over him. I sighed, for us and for his brief note:

"Silky long summer skirt, elastic waistband, front-button blouse. Flat shoes or sandals."

He had already made the "no underwear" condition. I remembered Monday night when he had fingered me, first pushing aside the crotch of my panties, them pulling them downward, pleasuring me into a haze of sexual heat. I could feel the heat rising now, remembering. My panties were damp.

After washing away the city's smudges, wrapped in a long robe, I finally ate my dinner. A glass of white wine was sitting poured for me in the refrigerator. Oh, Marilisa, I thought, you make me feel cared for... but I stopped my thought right there, by an act of will, feeling my loneliness for my mother and father, magnified by her generous caring. Her solicitude was a paradox, warming and saddening me all at the same time. Stupid Rand, I thought, so cold and hard, and so uselessly, when kindness would have won me over completely.

The wine made me sleepy. I was not eating enough these days to resist its effects. I would try to sleep late tomorrow, and then try on the outfit in my closet that seemed to fit Rand's specifications. If not, there would be time to shop for something suitable. Long silky skirts, long cotton skirts, even little ruffles on tiered long skirts, were being worn in the city. They were cool on warm days, they hid legs that might have imperfections, bruises from the gym or clumsiness, or legs en route to be shaved, or waxed into smoothness. The skirts covered the proverbial multitude of sins, but the elastic waist he wanted, while concealing my nakedness underneath, would be easy to pull off when he desired. The front-buttoning blouse would be easy to open. I was getting hotter thinking of his opening the blouse one button after another, down, down. No bra, as our agreement specified. Thank goodness my breasts were firm, jutting small peaks rather than broad and generous. Well, he seemed to like them last time.

Despite the wine's soothing, I was keyed up, and took a sleeping pill, hoping to collapse into dreamless sleep for a change. My little phone rang, making me smile again. "Hello, Bredon."

He could hear the effects of pill and wine beginning.

"Sleeping, Sis?"

"On the cusp, but I'm so glad to hear from you. Tell me what's happening."

"Really good news." He was laughing, lighthearted. "It looks like Rand is opting into the deal."

"Fabulous," I replied, all enthusiastic surprise. "When will it happen?"

"I think he'll start transferring funds at the end of this week. He said he was drawing on accounts that were not too 'noticeable' right now." Bredon and I laughed at the familiar ploy, our John and Mary Cole accounts, the kind of device that Rand was obviously using now.

This news that Rand had kept his word, and my brother's

hopeful happiness, released a sob. "Bredon, I'm so happy for you."

"Are you *crying?*" he asked me incredulously.

"Yes, can't help it. I'm so relieved." I knew he was too. "When did you find out?"

"Maybe an hour ago. Not even. And he said it with no explanations. I think he's embarrassed to have pulled out abruptly the way he did. But his family will still be nervous, or so he hinted."

"Nerves are part of a huge deal."

"*Really* nervous, Dray."

"And you too?" I wondered if he would tell me.

"Me too, a little bit." He laughed. "No sooner had Rand and I talked than the word seemed to be on the street. People are intrigued. We may get more investors."

Again I was sure it would have happened if Rand had just continued with Bredon for my sake. We could skip these sex games. Or were the sex games a planned bonus? I'd know tomorrow night.

"Bredon, honey, I'm fading…" I could barely talk.

"Sleep, Li'l Sis. Catch you later."

IX

Friday morning I managed to sleep until almost nine, having wakened at two AM, coming wide awake instantly, frustrated, knowing I would be up all night tonight. In the locked bathroom drawer with its special anti-steam lining, where I had stowed the Plan B and condoms, I kept all the drugs I had been given in the turmoil after the bombing. There were drugs for sleeping, for anxiety, for depression, a pharmacy for serenity that I had been grateful for. I swallowed the most benign of my sleeping pills, and then ate a plain cracker that seemed to accelerate the pills' effect, an accidental discovery I had made when I first used them. Sure enough I had been back asleep in twenty minutes.

I had set out the clothing I would wear tonight, adding a shawl-jacket in case it was cool, and to hide my obviously bra-less state. I chose closed sandals, a safer, cleaner bet for city streets, and would wear dark glasses and simply tie my hair back. I pulled a big black tote from a shelf, to hold a change of clothes.

I put a livery car number into my phone, for a company that I knew had women drivers. I planned to phone for a car to take me to the corner behind Rand's block, coming up the side street again. My Mary Cole credit card was in the skirt pocket along with cash for the ride and a tip. I would hang the security pouch around my neck under my blouse, to hold everything else valuable.

Marilisa phoned up, and yes, I would like breakfast. She brought coffee up, soft-boiled eggs, triangles of toast, cut-up melon and grapes, and The Times. I opened the door for her, glad to see her, glad for her normality and sanity and steadiness. I was in a long, light robe, my hair tied back, rested yet weary, emotions as taxing as exercise.

"Are you going out this morning?" she asked pleasantly, no

urgency. No mention of the note, the roses, my disappearances, just confining herself, ever tactfully, to daily routines. "If you won't be here, I'll send up the cleaners."

She gave me an idea. Rather than fretting or pacing or wandering different neighborhoods, I would try for the delights of the city, and put thoughts of tonight out of my head. "I'm going to a museum. They open at eleven, and I'll be gone until about three. I'll have lunch there," I told her. "But could you please leave an early dinner for me? Something simple, a sandwich, milk. By five?"

She nodded, sure, and said laughingly, "Oh, I love the way you eat lunch at dinner, and how often you eat dinner for breakfast." I was known to finish a roast chicken in the morning and have cereal and fruit at dinner time.

"Thanks." I returned her smile. The eggs were perfect, and how she got them cracked and into the dish while they were still hot, always amazed me. She used a kitchen towel, but nothing messy ever happened. I was still trying to accomplish this. She quickly set a place for me and arranged everything, including the paper, on the dining table.

"Do you need me to stay?"

"No, thanks Marilisa, this is fine." And with a smile, she was gone. I turned on the radio station that gave news and weather all day, relieved to hear the temperatures would be moderate tonight. Switching to the public classical station on FM, I broke pieces of toast into the eggs, looked at the stories filled with the conflicts and struggles of the world, skimmed the op-ed, and read the Arts page. Rand's museum trusteeship would be in tomorrow's early delivery of the Sunday section but I looked to see if any hint was there yet. Not finding one, I folded the paper open at the crossword puzzle, and put it in the magazine holder for later.

Breakfast finished, showered, dressed, I set out for the Morgan. I did not want to call any friends, too distracted for the normal conversations even of my most congenial peers. I especially did not want to talk about Bredon, and I did not want to mention Rand. So I followed my resolve to learn the public transportation system more thoroughly, going by crosstown bus to Madison Avenue, walking in the sweet air, the long blocks down to 36th Street. I had worn comfortable shoes, jeans and tunic, and the distractions of the scenery could for a few minutes at a time make me feel lighthearted and happy. Thoughts of Rand intruded; however I tried to turn them aside, remembering the touch of his hand between my legs, my body growing warm, pushing the images of him out of my mind.

At the museum I bought several books including the exhibit catalog from the gift shop, still struggling to keep myself distracted from thoughts of tonight. Rand, and whatever he was planning, kept slipping back into my imagination. When hunger drove me to the garden restaurant, I pressed my thighs together to quell the sexual itch I felt, and tried to focus on reading while waiting for the food, and then while eating it. After one last walk around the paintings I most loved, I made my way on foot and by bus back home. Sundown was a few hours away. I used my laptop as a diversion, answering emails, and using emails to answer texts, so much easier than thumbing my way along the phone's keyboard. There was a call from my school for volunteer sponsor-guides for the new freshman class. Robin and Dina and I had already planned to volunteer for this. I looked at the message list on my land line, no replies needed right now. Finally, I traced the electronic paths, one encryption after another, to Bredon's account for his current project. It showed money in the process of being transferred in. That had to be Rand's payment.

And now there was no more time. As usual, electronics ate up hours, and it was past six when I went to get dressed for the first night with Rand.

X

In the street I shifted the tote bag, which looked like the ones carried by foot travelers all over the city. Mine held a pair of jeans, running shoes, a t-shirt and plain white bra and panties, along with the pack of condoms at the bottom of the bag, a last hope. The cover-all shawl-jacket concealed my braless top, and would do double duty over the jeans when I came home.

I walked several blocks to the corner where I had arranged my car service pickup. It was almost sundown, the rush hour finished so that we made good time southward. The driver seemed to sense my preoccupation. Her look was kindly, but she did not try to start a conversation, and my mind was far away as she navigated the city streets neatly and quickly.

When we arrived I waited until she had driven away and turned a corner before I started walking up the street to Rand's gate. My sense of caution was in high gear. I felt shaky without any part of me actually showing any sort of tremor. In science class I had learned this feeling was a symptom of starvation. How suitable, how apt. I was in an emotional desert, no nourishing ground beneath me.

The quiet click of the gate, opening at my approach, seemed very loud on the dark, empty street. After I slipped in and started for the house, the metal gate seemed to lock behind me with an echo. I pulled the hidden purse from under my blouse and stuffed it onto the bottom of the tote bag, along with the credit card and cash from my skirt pocket. Rand pulled the door open as I got near. He was in shadow, outlined by his long robe which was narrow like a tunic, rather than an ample spa robe. The only light came from a doorway beyond the sitting room. He pointed us there, moving me ahead of him, his hand pressing my back and releasing a surge of heat and desire. His touch could evidently magically arouse me no matter where we were.

I tried to see everything as we came to the doorway, entering in the dim light, my heart thumping a bit, wondering if it was always set up this way. I had read enough erotic literature to recognize why he would have this strange mix of furniture, a setting for sexual fantasies. There was a narrow bed like a cot surrounded by pillows, a dresser, tables of unusual heights, a kind of love-seat chaise, a small sofa with unusually wide rolled arms, a wider bed with silk scarves looped around the head and foot posts, and a small table with various implements. I could just make out a wide short strap and a small cat o'nine tails. I could not see what Rand picked up from the table, as it was on the other side of him, but his other arm came around me to move me into an even further room. It was a luxurious bathroom, the raised tub filled with sweet-smelling foaming salts. The scent of roses. Beyond I could see the wooden enclosure of a sauna. He had retrofitted this old house into a love nest.

Putting down whatever he was holding, he turned me around, pulling off my shawl and pulling away the tote handles, tossing them into a corner with one hand, all the while pulling me closer with the other, and kissing me, his tongue tracing my lips in light circles, making my knees weak. He held me against him, one hand cupping my buttocks, the other unbuttoning my blouse, feeling my breasts between each button, his breath quick and hot. He tossed the blouse into the corner on top of the shawl, and I vaguely admired the precision of his blind aim. His robe came loose, and he pulled my hands up to lock them behind his neck, moving me back toward a small table that sat against the wall, leaning me against it while he pushed the elastic waistband of my skirt down to my thighs. One hand inserted between my buttocks, his other hand played with me. I was so wet, and my vision was hazy from desire.

He bent and pulled my skirt off and then my sandals, tossing them away. The room was steamy from the bath, but the chill made my nipples even harder, and Rand almost groaned as he pinched and caressed them, bending to give each one a quick sucking kiss.

I was barely able to stand, but he held me, and half-carried me to the tub, up the two steps, his own robe pulled off, and he got in first, bringing me in after him. The seat in the bathtub was just the right height for him to sit with the water at chest-level. His hands passed over my body as he parted my legs and positioned me to straddle his lap, facing him, his erection ready to enter me. I felt his penis pushing hard, and closed my eyes and clung to him, not caring if my nails dug into him, and with a great thrust he was inside me. I thought I would faint. I could see nothing, I closed my eyes, feeling a tiny pain as he thrust hard and exploded in me.

Our fluids floated upward, and a small pinkish staining of the water making him alert, and what seemed to be angry. "Are you a virgin?" he demanded, and when I remained silent, remembering our bargain, he said, "This is the one exception. Are you a virgin?" he repeated.

"I don't think so," I gasped. "I've done stuff…"

"Not enough stuff," he said roughly.

I knew I had had intercourse, but the boy I had been with was as young and inexperienced as I was, and he was small, his penis narrow. So maybe he had not completed the task after all.

Rand pulled me up and out of the tub. I saw two large robes on the shelf beyond us, but he pulled my wet body against him. He was all heat and desire, his eyes briefly thoughtful.

"If it hurts, I don't care," he said in a rough voice. "You'll have to put up with it."

I was in an aftermath of such throbbing, my breathing still rapid, I was not hurting, silently grateful that the pinch I had felt at his thrust had disappeared into orgasm.

His naked body still flush up against mine, he wrapped a large towel around us, binding us together, moving his chest slightly to feel my breasts against him, moving us backward into the sauna. The steam was pleasant, not with the distinctive fragrance of cedar, but like the bath, scented with roses. The sauna was made of pine or poplar, not that I cared.

He laid me face down on one of the benches, the towel under me, and quickly splashed cold water on my buttocks. Taking one of the small straps he had brought in, he held me lightly and used the strap on my buttocks, five short, sharp lashes.

"It hurts more when your skin is wet," he said.

Yes it did.

His voice was as quietly sharp, an edge of anger in his tone, and maybe cruel enjoyment. "I'll bet this is your first spanking."

It was.

He turned me face up, pulling the towel away, placing one of my legs straight along the bench and moving the other leg so that it hung over the side, and raised my arms above my head. "Stay that way," he said in a thick voice. Bending slightly, he traced his finger from my navel to my crotch, exploring me, then parting the lips. I saw he now had the small cat o'nine tails in his hand, and he flicked it against my openness, swift, stinging, brief. His erection was strong again, and he raised me, lifting me to a teak shelf, sitting me on it, my buttocks burning from the hardness of the wood after my spanking. He saw me wince, and smiled cruelly. I was even with the height of his penis, and wondered if he had had this shelf built just for this, as he parted my legs, and entered me again.

I was a bit sore now, and he felt the friction of it. He hesitated, perhaps wondering if I should be made to endure that pain too, but then he took a tube of lubricant and quickly worked it so that I was slippery. Pressing me back against the wall he held one hand over each of my breasts, squeezing them in rhythm with his thrusting, pinching my nipples, heady with his own lust, swinging in and out of me in long and lazy strokes. Suddenly his rhythm shifted to quick and hard, so that he came in a rush. A few moments' lingering, a last caress of my breasts, and he withdrew. Picking up the towel which had fallen to the floor, he wiped us both down, pulling me back to the tub for us to dip into the water, bathing away this new wetness. Next he put the spa robes on us, leading me back to where the beds were.

He laid me on the narrow cot. It was low, surrounded by pillows, and he knelt on them, bending over me, nibbling my breasts, sucking them, half whispering that my breasts would be very sore when he was done, working me with his clever hands, moving upward to kiss me with deep, penetrating French kisses, then running his tongue down my body to lick at me, circling my clitoris with his tongue and making me writhe with pleasure.

"Stay still," he commanded.

Well, that was our bargain. I held onto the sides of the cot as he called me his whore, and muttered bitter words, all because I had said no to him, because I loved Bredon more than even this crazy-making lust for him. I did not care what he said and where he touched me or how. Yes, for Bredon's sake, but also for my own lustful sake. A bargain made with a man whose first touch could start me toward a throbbing climax seemed an ironic gift.

He guided my hand to his erect penis, and I felt him swipe a line of lubricant into my palm. "Do what you did last time," he said, pleasure making his voice a thick growl. I repeated the technique Robin and I had learned, hearing him groan, and then he came over me, unable to wait any longer. "Spread your legs, wide, wider..." He pressed his hands outward on my inner thighs, entering me, thrusting, squeezing my buttocks, rearranging me and thrusting again. He pulled us both down onto the pillows, pressing me into them as he lowered his chest against mine, enough weight on his arms to keep from crushing me, but pinning me tightly as he rocked his hips fast and faster and gave a shout as he came. I could feel the spurting and the sense of fullness in his last thrusts. He stayed there as he grew soft, only slowly pulling out of me. He closed the robe over me as he rolled away, the pillows under us so soft, I think he dozed slightly and I felt myself drifting off in a cloud of pleasure and pain.

We woke to a small mantel clock striking two. Time was growing short. I don't think either of us thought we would sleep at all. Rand went into the sitting room, and somewhere beyond must have been a kitchen or pantry. I heard cups, a kettle. He came in with tea, herbal, fragrant. He had spooned honey into my cup, and I wondered if he had used it too. Silence prevailed. I sipped gratefully. Elderberry. It tasted wonderful.

He had been watching me, and as I finished he took my cup, setting it aside with his own.

"Come," he said, pulling me up, leading me now toward the bigger bed. We passed the strangely shaped piece beyond us that looked somewhat like a half-pear. It was cushioned all around, with little thongs and ribbons on the posts next to it. In answer to my silent, curious look, Rand said, "Next time," in the voice of a parent or principal who is saying that one's punishment is coming.

He laid me on the bed spread-eagle, spreading my thighs as wide apart as he could, and held a small vibrator against me, kissing me and then circling my breasts with his tongue.

"They look like gorgeous ice-cream cones," he said, "and oh, those sweet cherries at the top." My breasts were not the great size of women who have implants. They were an eighteen-year-old's breasts, high and very firm, pointy like the Balthus pictures, and sensitive to his every touch, kiss, lick, and tiny bite. I struggled not to squirm or moan. My buttocks throbbed from the spanking and my clitoris throbbed from the cat's blow and the vibrator, while his kisses drowned me with the pleasure his lips gave my mouth and my breasts, his tongue tracing the arc of my belly.

He used the lubricant on his penis, though I was very wet again. He swiped the lubricant between my buttocks, and took an object that he pressed into me. I gasped. It did not hurt, but it was a new sensation. "It's a butt plug," he said, recognizing that it was new to me. The plug had long leather strips attached to it, "so it doesn't get lost," he said and grinned, with a hint of lewd harshness. He moved his hand, fingers entering my vagina, his thumb on my clitoris, working me. My legs wanted to close over his hand, my arms moving downward from the spread-eagle position.

"Ah, you'll need some restraining." He gave a low laugh as he stopped to wrap the headboard scarves around each wrist, quickly securing my ankles with the scarves on the footboard posts. I was a naked X on the bed, and he gazed with satisfaction at the picture I made.

He laid his body over mine, his hands curving behind my hips and then between my buttocks, his penis entering me very deliberately, penetrating me very deeply; more, it seemed, than before. He stopped for a minute and reached over to the table, placing a long, flat object over my clitoris, a vibrator of a kind I had never seen, whirring, while his rhythm was languid but steady, and his breath grew more ragged, as mine did. I closed my eyes, wishing I could moan the way he did.

He took his time, and I had had a burst of orgasmic pleasure before he finished. He felt the change in my body, and I opened my eyes to see him, through my clouded vision, smiling almost smugly at my pleasure, his face quickly growing fierce, his eyes tightly closed as he moved toward climax. I became conscious of the chiming, again, from the mantel clock. It was almost time for me to leave.

He quickly undid the scarves, and I felt the release of pressure as he pulled the butt plug out. I went into the bathroom, glad to pee and to wash the fluids from between my legs, though the area was sore from Rand's rough sex. I stuffed the skirt and blouse into the tote bag and lifted the jeans out, pulling them on quickly, my crotch and buttocks smarting as they shaped themselves to my body. I fished out the cash, which I stuffed into my jeans pocket for the ride home. Retrieving my sandals and stuffing the other clothes into the bag, I pulled on the t-shirt, hung my security purse inside it, and slipped the shawl over me. When I emerged into the sitting room, Rand was also wearing jeans, his robe maybe in a laundry basket somewhere in the house.

He pulled me onto a hard chair across from him, smiling with satisfaction as I winced again. The spanking had been short but very effective. "I like your velvety fur," he grinned. "But I also want to see you without it."

I looked at him warily.

"I want you to get a Brazilian wax," he said, offhandedly. "No hair anywhere down there next time." He reached over to a small notebook and took a card from its inner pocket. "Go to this salon." The card simply said "Mme. Aldiva," with a Park Avenue address and phone number in the lower left corner. In the lower right corner were the words, "On the Mezzanine."

"She's expecting you on Wednesday, ten o'clock. I've told her that I'm sending you." Looking across the room at nothing in particular, in a tight voice, he said, "She'll have some other things for you to do." He ignored my questioning face. "Don't try to pay her or tip her. It's taken care of. I've told her you are Ms. Kaye. Leave as soon as you can after she's finished. You'll enter on Park, but you can leave on the side street." Now his look was stern. "She won't ask you any questions and she won't be talkative." I thought, no kidding, really?

I wondered how often he had done this before. Seeing my doubtful, studying look, he said, "My sister uses her." He grinned. "Sometimes her husband too."

I blinked at the information, though I knew men did these things. Seeing my face he said, "Not I. Not ever." So that was my answer but I was to be "Ms. Kaye." A funny play on words. "K" was the first letter of Balthus' real last name.

The sun was not quite up as I slipped away from Rand's house, phoning the car service as I went, walking a few blocks northward toward the pickup point I had asked for. And I thought about hair and waxing as the car drove through the sparse early traffic.

Many of the girls and women I knew had been waxed in all sorts of places. Hair was removed from their eyebrows, upper lips, underarms, "bikini lines," their legs, and for some whose body chemistry shifted to menopause, chin hairs that many found most mortifying of all.

Rand's body had downy, soft hair on his chest and stomach, down along the V that started below his navel, like a thin fur coat, beautiful, a light reddish brown. The stories of girls and women at my schools always had one story of a man whose rising curls of thick hair covered his back, chest, legs, even knees. Some hairy men who also had full beards, looked like bears covered in their winter coats. In high school, girls had competed with their funny stories of undressing with a man to find unexpected hair boiling out of shirts and trousers. I had seen enough pictures in books and online, to know how many ways hair covers the human body, or is barely there, like the gorgeous golden chests of Polynesian men. My brother and I had been spared the heavy growths of legs and arms, having inherited our mother's smooth-skinned body.

I also knew about waxing salons. Some women were extremely hairy, and thought themselves ugly for it, constantly fighting their own bodies with shaving, electrolysis, waxing, depilatories. Even where hair was supposed to be, on their heads, there was discontent. Whatever their hair type, my friends got their hair curled or straightened, bemoaning the fineness or the coarseness, friends of African descent in political issues with their hair as well, to straighten or not, and when and how. What I could easily understand was hair color and glamor. The tragedy of my parents deflected me from a lot of the typical adolescent preoccupation with appearance, and I had never been waxed nor part of a gym regimen, but I did return to using a salon, very expensive, very perfectionist, that produced eye-catching results to please my vanity.

My ruminations over these things ended as we pulled to the curb several blocks from my apartment. I walked from there in the cool morning air, glad for the shawl but feeling the warmth of summer on the soft winds that came and went. Home, I pulled off my jeans to relieve the pressure on my crotch and buttocks, and got water to take the first of the Plan B pills. Away from Rand, rationality had returned. He had been so deep in me when he came, and I was so lost in orgasm, I didn't care when I felt his warm fluids filling me. Now I cared very much, and made a note that I taped to my bathroom mirror, a "six PM" reminder to take the second pill.

Next I wanted to shower and to sleep for a while and put aloe vera lotions on my sore places. For the soreness between my legs, I would have to be content with Vaseline and cornstarch. I would check my messages later. The important thing was to rescue Bredon's project. Sitting in my panties at my computer, a soft pillow under me, I entered the passwords that led me to Bredon's account. The promised amount was there with the words, "transfer completed." I sighed, wondering where I would ever find a lover like Rand after his vengeful bargain was done. I shook my head, ah, well.

The Times had arrived, and I heard Marilisa open my door just widely enough to place the paper on a small table next to the doorway, softly closing it again and leaving. I remained quiet. My bedroom could not be seen from the front room, and she must have thought I was sleeping. I got the paper and looked at the Sunday sections that came bundled with the Saturday edition. Usually I looked first at the Magazine and the Book Review, but now I pulled out the Arts sections, quickly scanning the pages, and there was the story, Rand a museum trustee, a first for someone so young. He was thirty. Now I knew. Twelve years was a substantial age difference, as though it would ever matter now.

Marilisa had left some cut-up fruit and yogurt in the refrigerator, and there were some hard-boiled eggs, peeled and sitting in a small bowl. I poked down a couple of pieces of pineapple hoping the bromelain, the bruise-healing enzyme in the fruit, would help ease my soreness. I was tired, sad, feeling empty and lost. I reminded myself to be strong. In three years I had become far older than my age, learning to sustain myself with faith and the sheer will that faith supported. I said a little prayer to my parents for my brother, and felt better. I would get some sleep. Tomorrow was Sunday, and Bredon would be coming home.

XI

Ree and I took Bredon's car to get him at the airport. Carlos, his driver, had picked her up first, and I was happy to see her after so many times that we had just missed each other in one place or another. Ree was always generous about the time I shared with my brother, so open-hearted. I thought she was wonderful.

Bredon had met her in college, he about to graduate, she an entering freshmen. They had "clicked" on their very first date, and had been together ever since. She too was from an old, publicity-averse family, though she had been warm and sisterly toward me since the first time Bredon introduced her to our parents and me. We liked her immediately, and it was a lovely kind of re-play of our parents' romance. She was all that he wanted in a forever-love, and his feelings were so obviously reciprocated. After the bombing, as my brother steadied me, so Ree's presence, always in the background during the worst times, was a place of steadfastness and renewal for him.

I just wanted to see Bredon for a brief while, and then planned to disappear so that they could have some private time before he flew off again. They had insisted we have dinner together. I had agreed, with the proviso that I was up and gone before dessert. Ree had laughed when I said it, and realizing what I said, I laughed too. Their time together *was* dessert, and more.

I was grateful that Bredon had found Ree, and that my future sister-in-law never questioned me about boys or about anything in my life. My mother had been the same way, which led to my trust, and my openness with them. Not that there was much to say anyway, when it came to boys. I had not gone with one boy exclusively, as so many of girlfriends had done, and I was only vaguely interested in a couple of the smarter boys I had encountered in my circles.

So the talk Sunday night, at a dinner catered in Bredon's

apartment, was about his trip, the effects of Rand's opting into the deal, and stories of people he met and encountered by chance in the countries he had visited. He and I were always humbled by the dignified good humor of so many of the supposedly lower classes, in countries filled with poverty and struggle.

I could see that Bredon looked a lot better than he had when I'd left him at his office the past week. Private jet travel had spared him much of the tourist fatigue that comes with security lines and tight cabin quarters. Beyond that he looked happier, more satisfied and confident, which reassured me, and after the main course I took my leave, with quick hugs and kisses, despite their gentle protests that I stay longer. I was thankful that Carlos was there to drive me home. It was late, and it felt sane and peaceful to return home without having to slink into a back door in disguise. Yes, disguises could give privacy, but true freedom lay in being oneself.

Before I went to sleep that night I started a list of things to do in the next two days, since I had no idea what shape I would be in after Wednesday's waxing. I had only thus far looked at one video on the Internet, and did not know how long the post-waxing tenderness and pain would last. I would do more research tomorrow, but at the top of the list now I put "Plan B," for the coming weekend of unprotected sex with Rand. The thought of it, despite all my sensible fears, started a warmth between my legs. I got into bed and felt around my still-furry wetness, thinking of how he had circled my clitoris with his tongue, and it was not long before my fingers and my fantasies gave me an orgasm that put me into a sound sleep.

XII

I started my Internet research first thing after waking and having a cup of coffee. To deal with the crazy desire that Rand could make me feel, I chided myself into remembering how wicked he was to demand this unprotected sex. The graphic pictures we had seen in sex education classes in high school brought back the dangers all too clearly. I shivered at the thought that he had given me some sort of disease. Using the Internet to bring up pictures of their effects, could still make me squirm with their close-up details of sores, rashes, and warts. The pain and burning and long-term consequences were elaborated in print beside each set of pictures. Oh, ugh, oh I felt so crazy and disgusted over the whole situation I had agreed to.

Then I remembered last night, and the relaxed confidence Bredon had shown, the glow between him and Ree that might have been absent if huge financial losses loomed over him. It renewed my resolve to match Rand at his sex games, and enjoy it, the ultimate irony. I tried not to think of other women he had slept with, and what he had been left with.

I realized that today was one week since first meeting Rand, and so much had happened that the week seemed like a hundred years of days. We had had one night of true passion, which now had disappeared into a sexual bargain that would include being stripped of my adult woman's furry growths. I wanted to know in detail what was going to happen, clicking avidly through lists of sites and videos. Knowledge is power. Yes, sure.

There were lots of online reports mostly saying that waxing hurt. Some blogs were arguments with each other about how much pain and how much after-effect resulted from waxing. They said the first time hurts the most. Oh, yay, just what I needed to read.

A video demonstrated how a woman waxed at home, and

how she eased the pain. I sighed as I watched her press each painful area she had just finished waxing, pulling the cloth strips off various parts of her crotch, then waxing inside her buttocks. I found myself clenching my teeth, resigning myself once again to the bargain I had made with Rand, and the whole reason for all of this.

Next I steeled myself and looked for videos of what I was sure Rand planned to do. The formal term was "sodomy," which in modern language is anal sex. The first videos were only a bit graphic, more hint than actual visual instruction. There were varied posted comments about "taking it in the rear": hating it, tolerating it, getting used to it, using it as a trading card, loving it to the point of orgasm.

At my high school while I boarded, I had only met one girl who admitted having had anal sex, and she said it was enjoyable. But she was a rather ditzy girl who also thought that marijuana was the kindest thing she could do to her body. I was repelled by the cloying smell of marijuana, making other girls think my sense of smell was warped. They dismissively ignored me in their many detailed conversations fueled by the tongue-loosening effects of alcohol, weed, and whatever else was being consumed during post-lights-out gatherings in dank places in the school basement.

My reserve outweighed peer pressure as I remembered my parents' warnings about compromising videos that might haunt me forever. It amazed me that lovers posted naked pictures of each other, or sent pictures of their genitals. Exhibitionism was not my thing, and some of the girls at school were starting to send their naked pictures to their boyfriends. I thought it was stupid, and outrageous, I who was steeped in conversations about privacy that had started in early childhood. I was such an outsider to all of this. When I told my parents I preferred living at home to boarding, they transferred me to a private day school in the city. They did not question me closely about my choice, my wise mother seeming to sense that a day school was a happier place for me to be.

So I was left with no girlfriend to tell me her experience, and the two boys I knew who were gay would probably have been horrified if I questioned them about men's lovemaking techniques. The great film about two cowboy lovers, and the original story, did not help much either. The thought of wading through gay porn and trying to order it online was daunting. It was the Internet or nothing.

On the Net I found all sorts of bad videos and skewed explanations, long preachy discussions with no real information, and simply not enough graphic detail without spending hours exploring porn sites. I saw enough to learn that the woman should be on top at first, and I concluded that several tubes of lubricant, at minimum, were the true necessity for successful penetration. Picturing Rand's beautiful penis made me feel the now-familiar sexual itch between my legs, and the butt plug he had used had not hurt. But that was not a penis thrusting, as the women described it in the videos. Oh, God.

While I was at it, I did research into an IUD as a possible substitute for another round of Plan B. But I did not plan to have sex with anyone after this next weekend with Rand, and I still had the trusty three-pack of condoms. Although the IUD was the best and safest birth control, it didn't protect against diseases. And the IUD had strings that came down into the vagina and were supposed to be wrapped around the cervix, out of the way. I was afraid that I would be unlucky and have the possible side-effect of loosened strings that would hang down. I could imagine Rand feeling them and saying I had broken our bargain for raw sex. So I opted to stay with Plan B. I knew there were lots of counterarguments to my decision, but my mind was made up. What I still needed, though, was medical information I could trust, and so I put in a call to Ren's office and within a minute I was told to come in on Tuesday morning, first thing. I knew the receptionist had recognized my name.

As I continued to scroll through what seemed to be endless and often useless sites, messages came in from Robin and Dina. I quickly answered, saying I was in the midst of family stuff and that we could start to make plans next week. I was looking forward to resuming something that resembled a normal life, but even as I thought of it, I wondered if we should go out to meet some guys in the hope that we could find interesting male bodies and minds, and maybe even some delicious unvengeful sex. Rand had set the bar very high, and his name alone, as I thought about it, set me itching "down below", as they say.

At nine A.M. the next morning I was in Ren Harris' office. I loved that our doctor was Bredon's friend and my special godfather. He and Brendon had been friends all through school, teammates and study partners, of one mind about justice, and had stood with Bredon against the bullies, to defend Tomàs. Ren and Bredon were only children until I was born. Then he was so fascinated and taken with this new baby girl in his best friend's arms, he quickly saw me as his own surrogate baby sister.

"Dr. Harris will see you now," his receptionist said with a smile. Her name was Annie, and she was a youngish woman who thought Ren and I and my brother were cousins. We had never corrected that impression. Being family simply made everything easier.

Inside, I gave his hand a little squeeze, and sat down. He quickly assessed how I looked, my coloring, my demeanor. He was holistic, looking at the total patient, able to assess their state of mind and state of being, partly through his science, partly through the intuitiveness that makes some doctors into geniuses. Rendell Carter Harris was such a doctor, and the many plaques, awards, and citations of excellence bestowed upon him over the years, attested to that. He was a doctor's doctor, the one whom other doctors called when they were stumped by a case. He had a stunning record of finding causes and suggesting treatments that had eluded even brilliant colleagues.

As Bredon's best friend, their relationship always close, Ren knew some of the risks and perils Bredon faced in the financial world. They confided in each other, I knew, and Ren was going to be Bredon's best man when the wedding finally took place. But I did not mention anything of Bredon's current deal, for I did not know how many details Bredon had shared, and I certainly would not tell him of the bargain I had made with Rand. I knew, for all the medical confidences he kept, that his outrage at Rand would lead him at least to hint about it to Bredon, and the two men, knowing each other so deeply and for so long, seemed to sense each other's secrets. If my brother knew any of it, all our worlds would explode. So I told Ren that I was there to ask him about a new boyfriend, leading him to believe I was asking about a boy my own age.

At first Ren was pleased that I had a young man in my life, but looked dubious about it after I told him, haltingly, reluctantly, that we were lovers, and that he wanted me to be waxed. The websites I had waded through had not mentioned infection from waxing, but all the science I knew told me that there were risks. Ren nodded yes, there were.

"Are you sure you want to do this?" he asked, perhaps surprised that a young man had initiated the request, and then that I had agreed to it. He knew my rebel self. When I did not answer he said, "It will hurt, for starters." He could not avoid the shadow of a grimace at the thought of wax pulling hair off those delicate parts. He looked at me. "You *have* to do this, I take it." His eyes were warm, a sympathy he could allow to show because of our closeness.

I just nodded. The bargain with Rand was clear, and I was determined not to give him any excuse to back out of helping my brother. If his fantasy was my body without its downy covering between my legs, to look like a girl before puberty, so be it. Balthus would have been proud.

Ren must quickly have surmised something about the situation, because he did not try to dissuade me further. He studied me, which I pretended to ignore, and gave very serious instructions. "Make sure they use antiseptic technique. Lots of washing, lots of alcohol, lots of sterile cloths. A person getting waxed can develop a folliculitis, a staph infection, the hair follicles can become infected. Come see me afterward if you suspect the least trouble. And use these wipes when you get home," he said, quickly filling out a prescription in his neat, un-doctorly hand. "They might burn, but then, as the burning passes, you can use this," and he wrote another prescription for a numbing gel.

He could not resist a further question. "You *are* practicing safe sex, yes?"

"Of course," I lied with amoral nonchalance. "And thank you, Ren." His look softened, my gratitude and relief obvious to him. He gave me a quick hug and peck on the cheek, and then walked out with me. His waiting room was empty. He had scheduled me way off his regular hours.

How I wished there really was someone in town with whom I had a deep and good friendship. I wished Robin was already back, or that I could be with her as she dealt with difficult family issues. Her situation resonated with me. She might be seeing some much-loved relatives for the last time, and I pictured her, coping with mortality, coping with her parents who would try to put a positive face on the end of a life. I sighed, knowing she too wished I could have been with her. But to her parents, I would have been an intruder. Understandable, but I missed my friend.

Preoccupied with these thoughts I reached the lobby of Ren's building, mirrored elevators, cool gleaming marble. The main elevators were programmed to skip the middle tier of floors which included Ren's office. That middle tier held several luxury medical practices that were only accessible by referral. There were discreet patient entrances for them, a reserved private corridor, and elevators that went straight to those floors.

Most of the practices were high-end plastic surgeons who treated not only rich private patients, but also media stars and public figures. They did not want their fans or constituencies to know how their faces maintained a kind of perpetual youth. But Ren's office was for another high-priced clientele: those who concealed all illnesses because it might be interpreted as weakness, an opening to financial enemies or competitors. Foreign officials came here too, to hide their medical conditions from their countrymen and to avoid coups by younger, stronger, healthier aspirants to power.

To my proud pleasure, Ren also did much pro bono work in the city's clinics for the poor; but his places of work were ever changing as the poor were chased to ever more marginal or remote areas of the city, as the price of living went up and up. Movie-star handsome, Ren had been married while in medical school, his young wife dying before she was thirty from an aggressive form of breast cancer. He watched helplessly, his medical arts useless to help the woman he had loved since college days. He and Bredon had double-dated with their future wives, another bond that cemented their friendship.

After a long period of mourning, there had been a succession of women, many of them kind and loving. Ren had introduced me to them over the years, but had never moved to remarry. I wondered if he would find happiness with a wife again, and hoped he would, such a good and fine man.

I was caught in these reveries as I walked along Fifth Avenue, passing St. Thomas Church, its great flags waving, visitors and tourists entering and leaving, some clustered on its steps. I was tempted to go in, but as I hesitated I saw Rand standing in front of me, watching me, his ever-present black car at the curb. I wondered what he was doing here, what he did that led him to so many places at so many different times of the day. He looked at me with a mixture of anger and desire, and I could feel my heart thumping again, the intractable chemistry of him out of my conscious control. My body wanted him, there was no denying the slight pulse that I imagined I could feel against my panties.

I had been walking north, but decided to turn around. Would I always be heading downtown when he was in the picture, I wondered. Maybe I would go back toward the theater district, perhaps buy tickets for a show for tonight, anything to get away from him though I also did not want to. His body language had been one of waiting to see whether I would walk toward him, and when I turned away, he came quickly up beside me and matched my pace as I walked along the busy avenue.

I was frantic that my brother's many acquaintances and social spies not see us, so I shook my head to shake him away, and he grinned, and fell back. I practically ran to the corner to cross as the light changed, taking a side street and heading west. Few people were on the street. The lunch crowd from the office buildings had not yet emerged, and it was too early for the vendors whose bicycle-driven carts would line the curb, with various ethnic foods to sell to the hungry workers.

My heart was feeling sad and tired from having seen Rand, from the futility of my feelings, and that he saw me as whoring myself to him for money. I was sure he thought my only motive was money, to protect my brother, yes, but also to protect my own fortune. He had no idea how my brother had insulated my assets against any possible claim from his dealings.

I reached the Times Square area, its great steps at 46th Street, the wild billboards in their looping creativity. I did not want to call Bredon and interrupt his last hours with Ree, since his plane would be leaving in the late afternoon. Wanting simply to connect with him, I called the private line at his office that only he answered, knowing it would go straight to voice mail. I left an "I love you," "Hello to Ree," and "Be safe traveling" set of messages. It calmed me to have spoken aloud even to the digital ether.

I turned back east on 46th Street to my refuge, St. Mary's, and arrived in time for the beginning of the midday sung Mass. The clouds of incense and the music soothed my soul. I took my favorite place at a front pew where I could have full view of the altar. As the gorgeous liturgy started, my heart quieted. Losing myself in the rite, my eyes more closed than open, I let the old pattern of prayer and song and reading and prayer and consecration absorb me and replace the ache in my heart with calm and familiar consolations.

But when the people were summoned to the altar rail for Communion I almost said, "Oh!" out loud, for Rand was sitting at the end of the pew, watching me. I was angry, my heart feeling violated in a way so different from our sexual entanglings. The privacy of my religious life was a steadying foundation for me, and it had been breached by an interloper. I knew anyone was free to worship anywhere, but he had not come into church for the Mass. If he was so taken with me, why not help Bredon, and be my lover without the games and rules he had made?

He saw my eyes flash as I stood to leave the pew, and he got up and stood back as though to let me go first. But he did not come up to the altar with me, and when I returned to my seat he was gone. My heart, which had been pounding between indignation and desire, finally calmed. I decided to use the 47th Street exit, but as I emerged I saw his black car parked across the street, his window rolled down enough for me to see him. How did he know I would exit this way, I wondered.

In that minute, an angel sent a cab right down the street, and I hailed it and was inside quick as a wink. The traffic down 47th Street was, for a change, lighter than usual, and I had the cab take me uptown to my apartment, paying quickly with my card, and running inside to the welcoming doorman. I wished I could call Robin and tell her everything, but even if I could call her, I could not tell her much of anything, of this bargain, of the reasons for it. One slip, even by an innocent comment, and all this intrigue and slinking about, the spankings and the raw sex, would have been for naught.

As I came into my study niche I found my message light on. The data read-out said it was Rand. The agreement was no contact except our weekends, and here he was violating all these rules he had made, while I had no recourse. He still was in control, he had the money to rescue my brother. So I pressed the button and his voice came over, quietly taunting.

"Are we into Magdalene mode?" he said, referring to the woman who was wrongly considered a prostitute. People think she was the woman caught in adultery, that she was a whore. But in the scriptures it said she was a friend of Herod's steward's wife. That's like being the friend of the CFO's wife in a corporation, and it is highly doubtful that a woman of such high standing in ancient Israel would consort with a prostitute.

I used the special text keyboard on my study phone and sent a text reply: "Do read the scriptures again." The old bigotry, the old misreading, the old assumptions of whoredom. I no longer cared, and pressed "Erase" to send his message into oblivion.

XIII

Wednesday. Today was the day. I pressed my thighs together, trying not to imagine the pain of being waxed and thereby making it worse. I had done some quick research using Bredon's data bases, and "Madame Aldiva's" building was another family holding that Rand and one of his sisters controlled. It was a twin to the building Rand had shown me, where his apartment was, before we went to the restaurant and to the house where we made love... The thought made my breath start to come more quickly.

I forced myself to focus on the Park Avenue building. The floor plans and interior sketches showed rear apartments on the mezzanine that ringed the inner courtyard. I saw the back door traced in broken lines, the exit Rand had mentioned.

I decided to wear something that would, I hoped, cover up my identity. Going into the secret closet, I extracted a long black raincoat and voluminous headscarf, along with large wraparound dark glasses. I would be a modest Arab woman. Raincoats were their standard outdoor outfit these days, even in the heat. A white raincoat would be better for the season, but many women wore black in summer too. Such outfits were common enough in New York to be ignored, and that was my aim. I wore low, comfortable shoes and a long, loose tunic-and-skirt outfit. The spanking last weekend had left me sore enough when I pulled on my jeans. I could just imagine how I would feel after the waxing. No jeans this time.

I put my valuables in my under-the-shirt pouch, holding the raincoat and scarf, the dark glasses pushed up onto my head. My small phone was in my skirt pocket, and there was cash in the raincoat pocket for the cab I would take. Going out the rear entrance, one of the three janitors on duty waved to me. Bredon had hired them, and rewarded them well for their care and silence. They were older, family men, two of them immigrants, all of them glad for jobs that had low status but high rewards for the way they helped tenants avoid notice, publicity, and on occasion, reporters. One of them had a special nose for private investigators. I wondered how many marriages he had saved, how many scandals he helped avert. The nuns at Robin's Swiss convent school would have said he was headed straight to heaven when he died. Of course, the nuns would have assumed that he worked only to protect the sinless innocent. Robin and I had held a giggling and sometimes screamingly laughing discussion of the nuns' own innocence about matters like this. In truth, we were both thankful that such women existed in the world. They had given Robin a safe, happy place, however stern and full of rules the school had seemed from the outside. No religious practice was imposed on her, nor upon any of the girls. They could opt to pray with the nuns, or keep their own private religious practices, if any at all. The girls had been treated like daughters, and their grateful charges and their families had endowed the school in hugely generous amounts in thanks for their goodness and for the fabulous education they had provided. I missed Robin. I missed everyone I loved, and felt very alone as I headed for a session that was sure to be filled with grimaces and pain.

Once I was out of sight of the janitors, in a nook where no cameras scanned, I slipped on the raincoat and scarf, pulling it forward, putting on the large dark glasses, and quickly exiting. I walked to the next avenue and hailed a cab, giving the address, paying in cash when we arrived.

The Park Avenue median was newly planted with flowers, and Madame Aldiva was in the old, beautifully preserved behemoth of a building on the northbound side of the street. No one was about as I entered the building, the doorman holding the door open for me but narrowing his eyes, the concierge coming forward.

"Ms. Kaye for Madame Aldiva," I told him in a low voice. At that, the doorman relaxed and the concierge practically whisked me to a two-person elevator off behind a pillar next to his concierge storage room. Once I was inside the elevator, he reached in and pressed "M." I nodded and he backed away since he had kept the door open by reaching in. I pressed "M" again, and was quickly lifted to the mezzanine level, which had a balcony on the small interior court. The first door on the balcony opened, and a woman as tall as I, but of older, womanly bulk, reached out to take my hand and guide me inside. The concierge must have signaled her because I could see the glowing amber light next to the wall phone near the door. She locked the door behind us, quickly pressing the button under the light so it went out.

"Come in, come in," she said kindly, her heavy accent perhaps Russian and something else, her smile warm. She held my hand until we reached the sitting room, and then she helped me off with the raincoat, and I removed the scarf and glasses with relief.

"Madame Aldiva," I started to say, but she said, "Call me Reza."

"This is my first waxing…" and again she cut me off.

"Yes, I know." Her large brown eyes held humor and sympathy. I was relieved to see no hint of sadistic pleasure. "Come into this room," and she led me to a far door that opened into a room that looked like a surgical office, the table covered completely with white paper sheets. A counter on one wall, running almost the length of the room, held a variety of lotions and other liquids. A heating device glowed, and next to it, sealed boxes of strips, and bars of wax. At the end of the counter was a sink with hands-free dispensers for liquid soap and paper towels.

Ren would have been pleased at the cleanliness, I thought, though I was repelled at seeing all of this. Reza saw my look.

"We do this the very clean way," she said, taking my hand again. "Please, take off your skirt and sit on the table." She motioned me to a chair, also draped in white paper sheets, but my skirt was elastic-banded, so I slipped it down and laid it on the chair.

"Good," she said, making no effort to cover me as a doctor would. I was simply naked from the waist down.

"Come," and she guided me onto the table, gently pushing at me until I was lying down. "Wait," she said.

She went to the sink, washed thoroughly, and pulled on a fresh pair of thin plastic gloves such as beauticians use. At the warming element where wax had been heating, she laid a long white strip on top of the wax and let it sit there while she turned back to me. With a washcloth that was warm and had the antiseptic soap on it, she quickly ran it around my crotch, lifting my knees and reaching back between my buttocks. Another cloth with warm water only, rinsed me off. She gently toweled me dry, and used a small hairdryer on a low setting to dry the area completely.

Then it began, the first strip laid atop what is called the "Mound of Venus," the wax warm but quickly hardening to cool, and then she held my skin taut with one hand, pulling the strip with the other, the hair neatly lifting off, and it hurt like hell. "Oh, God," I murmured.

"Be patient, I will be quick," she said, and I could see she meant it.

The next fifteen minutes were a blur of cloth strips, pulling, pain, until all the front of me was smooth, and then she had me turn over, and quickly did inside each buttock.

With sterile gauze dipped in some kind of clear antiseptic liquid, she wiped down all the areas she had waxed. I looked down at myself, seeing a hairless nakedness I had not seen since I was twelve years old.

"It will hurt less the next time," she reassured me.

Like hell there will be a next time, I thought.

After she dried off the latest lotion with the hairdryer on a low setting, she dipped another pad of sterile gauze into another liquid and dabbed it on, so that I felt some relief.

"This is a numbing cream," she said. "And the soreness should be gone by tonight."

"What if I soak in ice water?" I mused aloud.

"It might help." She held my arm as I sat upright, and brought me my skirt to pull on. I was glad I had thought to use this outfit. Oh, God, I thought again.

"There is one more thing I must give you," she said quietly. She had a small box in her hand. "These are laxatives. Take them tomorrow afternoon. They should work by the evening. After that, only drink clear liquids, apple sauce, gelatin."

I looked at her, wondering if she knew why Rand had ordered the laxatives and this diet.

She knew.

She thought for a minute and said, "Sit on the table again, pull your skirt off." She brought a bottle of aloe vera gel. "I am going to put this on, it will be very wet for a while, but it will help." She was right. It was soothing. I put my skirt back on, and went into the front room. She had put a bottle of the aloe vera into a small plastic bag for me, tying the carry handles so that the bottle did not show.

"Thank you," I said. She had showed absolutely no reaction to my nakedness, and no expectation that I would be embarrassed or shy. I had to admire her, so matter-of-fact, after what had to be countless vulvas and buttocks and penises and hairy chests, and who-knows-what, that she had seen.

She seemed to read my thoughts and smiled. "You are very easy to take care of," she said. "Very brave."

I didn't feel brave, just relieved that it was over. I pulled the scarf over my hairline and pulled the belt tightly on the raincoat. She led me to a rear door that went one flight down to the back exit, and watched me as I descended. I put the dark glasses on and opened the door, finding myself on the side street, walking to the next street to hail a cab to go home. I was feeling sore and I dreaded taking the laxatives, but I would do it.

When I got home, ditching the coat and scarf as I entered my building, I changed and went to a pharmacy to get the antiseptic wipes and numbing lotion that Ren had prescribed. I used the wipes though they burned, and then slathered on aloe vera. When it finally dried, I began using the numbing lotion. It felt very strange, but I was going to hide out and sit on pillows, and put wet washcloths in the freezer to make cool compresses. I put towels under me on my sofa, and gathered unread New Yorkers, mail, and newspapers, and settled in to read, and heal.

When Bredon called late in the afternoon I was already feeling soothed, lazy, happy to have caught up on some reading, and he heard that contentment, and was reassured. All the rest of the day, and the next, I stayed in the apartment, music on or some television, mostly reading, sitting on soft pillows to go online, hermit practices until I was no longer sore from the waxing.

On Friday morning I woke to a sense of wary anticipation. Tonight with Rand – the thought perversely starting the warmth and throbbing that the idea of him seemed always to produce. I pictured his penis, that pleasure stick, and wryly thought, if only our coupling were simply for pleasure – and maybe even for love.

Thinking of him put me into fantasies. Although I had never before wanted to do it, I thought about what it might be like to run my tongue over his penis, to pull back the foreskin and slide my hand along the shaft of him, as though to masturbate him, but making him as wild as his lovemaking made me. Not that it was "lovemaking," strictly speaking. It was sex, a bargain, a monetary exchange that he hated me for. I sighed. Sighing was becoming such a frequent habit, so much to sigh over.

I was drinking the delicious coffee that Marilisa had prepared and set for brewing last night. She had been like a sylph, breezing into my apartment on Thursday night, her visit far later than usual, seven-thirty, a long day for her. She said nothing when she saw all the used washcloths piled in the bathroom. The compresses and creams and aloe vera had done their work. I could hide the creams, but not the cloths. She would have to draw her own conclusions. I noticed that she looked tired, the slightest wisp sticking out from her always neat hair.

"I don't need anything, Marilisa, do get some rest," I told her.

"No, no, I'm fine," she said, but I could see her fatigue in her quiet manner. She had set the coffeemaker over my protests, put some fresh washcloths and towels in the bathroom, and at my urging, left it at that. She had days like this, demands on every side. And then she had days that were relatively easy, many of her "concierge group" going on extended vacations or to homes or apartments in other parts of the country or the world. I knew that Bredon had encouraged her to take at least one course, even online, from the community college. She had never had a chance at higher education before Bredon hired her. Maybe she had begun. I wondered if she would tell me. Some people were invigorated by college courses. Others who were not used to it, found the focused thought of a college course more tiring than physical labor. I had heard people say it about themselves, and I did not doubt its truth.

As though I had summoned her by thinking about her, I heard her little bell at the door. "May I come in?" she called.

"Yes, come in, the coffee is delicious, have some," I said as I took The Times from her hand and saw her little cart behind her. I always offered, she never accepted. But I was determined to keep trying. Maybe one day she would actually sit down and have a cup with me.

"A package just came for you," she said. What self-discipline she had. No look of curiosity, no change of expression, the same matter-of-factness that Reza had shown. Oh, the women who tend the world. What can surprise them?

She put the package on the dining room table, checked to be sure there was ample breakfast fare, and smiled her good-bye. I knew better than to ask who had delivered the package. It had to be Tom.

It was a traditional rectangular box that the Fifth Avenue stores used to pack dresses or sweaters, the kind of box that gets wrapped as a present during the holidays. It had a sealed envelope on top with my name in the same block letters as last time, and was taped in such a way that no one could read it without damaging the shiny white wrapping paper.

Tearing away the paper I opened the box, and there laid out neatly was a complete outfit: the white blouse, pullover sweater, red fine wool skirt, an underskirt that I didn't know where he found, the shoes, the knee socks, the white cotton panties that a pre-adolescent girl would wear, like Thérèse in the Balthus painting. I looked at the note inside the envelope: *Wear these on Friday night. Nothing else.* Which meant, as usual, no bra. And this time, my hairless sex would be covered by young girl white panties.

Even his note could arouse me. I felt a major throb of fear and pleasure from between my legs up to my navel. I touched myself, feeling my own wetness and sensitivity. He had not put his usual "R" at the end of the message. I wondered if he was going to be very rough tonight, and thought, he probably will.

Seeing the cloudy sky I checked the weather report on my laptop. Rain. I pulled out a thin traveling rain cape that had armholes and buttons, that I would use to cover the outfit when I went to meet Rand, and it would cover me on my return. I got the tote bag, and packed a non-wrinkling travel dress, underwear, and closed sandals to wear back home when this night of sex, and his vengeance were over. I was sure he was going to use me angrily. Revenge for my choosing Bredon. He was fixated on punishing me for it. I checked Bredon's account online, and the final transfer had already been made. Rand had put the money in early, a surprise.

I checked the calendar again. No hope of an early period. It would be Plan B again. No need to pack tampons. But I put the condoms into the bag, still hoping he would at least use them if he wanted to take me in the rear. The pills Madame Aldiva had given me had done their work by last night. No untidiness, no embarrassment, but the anticipation of tonight's pain and pressure made me squirm.

I found Rand's body to be a powerful aphrodisiac, and desire fought with reluctance as I tried to imagine tonight. I wondered how much of his true self was being revealed on these two weekends. Did he devise that room full of beds and furniture just for our sexual bargain? Was it all to get back at me for refusing him? So much heat and anger when he had sex with me, when he kissed me and felt me everywhere and pleasured me. But he excited and aroused me so mightily, I ignored his anger and everything except his touch and scent.

Last week, at one point the push of his penis sent me into such a state that my vaginal muscles had grabbed him as he was inside me, making him gasp in surprise. I had pretended to ignore his reaction, remembering my bargain to be silent and his determination not to pleasure me, my attempt to keep him from realizing how sensual and exciting it was to have sex with him. But of course he realized. The chemistry between us could not be ignored or denied.

Getting to his place tonight would be a repeat of last week, and thank goodness knee socks were being worn by young women as part of funky outfits. The rain cape would make my outfit a strange one, but in New York, even the strangest ways of dressing were ignored more than noticed. How Rand had got shoes that fit me so well was a mystery, or maybe not. He had the power to compel personal shoppers to reveal sizes. I knew Bredon's power to get information from people. Rand's power was at least as great, and no doubt greater.

So the shoes were comfortable for my walk to the pick-up point for my car service, and as the sun was going down I was in Rand's park, approaching his house, dressed like a defiantly naughty girl.

XIV

He let me in quickly, the room dimly lit, closing the door behind me and throwing an additional bolt. I had not seen that last time, and he said as though reading my thoughts, "Yes, it's new. Extra privacy." Matter-of-factly, as he took my bag and put it on a small table, and unbuttoned my rain cape, laying it over the bag. He took my hand and led me to the next room with its beds and sex furniture. The place smelled fresh; all the beds looked newly made up. I wondered what crew he had, and what he paid, to buy so much cleanliness and silence.

He turned to look at me, surveying me up and down, satisfied that I somehow looked like the naughty adolescent girl who might not keep her knees together, so that a boy could look up her skirt and see the places he would love to explore and penetrate. He had the bad boy look in his eyes, and mischief. He was enjoying himself, and I pretended to look elsewhere, but I was feeling the thrill of being with him again. I wanted to press my hand against his rising erection, but held myself in check as he sat me on a high wooden stool, guiding my foot to its rung for me to climb onto it, turning me to face him, my back against the wooden back rest. No cushions here.

He pushed my knees apart, my skirt still covering them, and he pushed the skirt back, lifting it, looking at the cotton panties. He slipped his fingers behind the crotch piece and felt along my bareness and openness, feeling my moisture as he rubbed his fingers flat, up and down.

"Oh, how naughty," he said, grinning. "So smooth," he mocked, "bad little girl."

He ran his hand over my hairlessness, lightly pinching the lips, reaching back to feel inside my buttocks. It excited him, as his ever-faster breathing told me. My own breathing was more rapid, my body thrilling as he touched me, at the pinches, at his hot skin and the heat of his hands as he held me.

He pushed the skirt higher, so that it was bunched at the top of my thighs, and he positioned my knees even wider apart. Then taking a few steps back, studying my bad girl pose, he quickly undid his trousers, releasing the hard erection that had risen, and undid the buttons of his already half-unbuttoned shirt. In a minute, trousers and shirt off, no underwear, barefoot, he reached behind me for a thin men's robe, and put it on, leaving it open and loose. It looked like a desert robe, so masculine, so exciting. His eyes were clouded with desire and sexual purpose, the look on his face making me want to faint with anticipation of what was about to happen.

Coming close against my knees, he pulled me up toward him, his penis pushing the crotch of my panties aside as he slid into me, a few quick thrusts, pulling the back of the stool forward to press me against him as he thrust, and then slipping his hand between us, pressing his thumb onto my clitoris, pushing and releasing, then doing it again, and then withdrawing his hand, his penis thrusting quickly, hotly, and I felt him swell and come, an explosion of heat and wetness filling me.

I was throbbing, biting my lower lip, feeling his heart pounding. He backed out of me slowly, pulling me down from the stool as he did so. He slipped his hand into my panties and pressed and played with me, a painful pleasure for my own swollen sex. I could hardly stand, and he pressed me close to him, drawing me over to the high bedstead. I was still breathing hard. He leaned me against the bed.

"Lift up your skirt," he ordered. I did so, controlling my shaking hands. The skirt had an elastic band, and he tucked the hem into the band so that the front of the skirt was completely raised. "Now the slip," and I lifted it. "Tuck it into the waist," and I did that.

"Now pull your panties down, slowly."

I reached up to the thick waistband of the panties, starting to lower them, and when I got them to the tops of my thighs I was about to bend to continue to lower them, but he stopped me, holding my hands. He reached down and pulled the panties to the middle of my thighs. He ran a finger along the crease of my sex, and then he ran his hand over the smoothness of me. Taking one of the hand towels from the bedside table, he passed it between my legs, catching the wetness that had now flowed out of me from his coming. He rubbed at the stickiness on my thighs, grinning, giving my clitoris little pinches between towel strokes. My knees were weak from the pinches.

Next to the hand towels on the table were other things, some I recognized from last time, some new. He saw me look at them, and nodded a few times.

"Yes, I think before we go any further, you are going to need a good spanking again. I didn't really spank you properly last time. This time, we'll be thorough." He turned me around and pulled my skirt and slip up. "Assume the position, as they say," he told me, and he guided me to bend and lie face down on the bed, my buttocks bare, my feet no longer touching the floor. He had the skirt completely up, the panties still around my thighs.

"We can start this way," he said nonchalantly, and I saw him take a bottle and drop some liquid into his hand, then passing it over my bare behind. "Oil," he said. "No permanent marks. And more chastisement," he said the word lingeringly, mockingly. He ran the oil between my buttocks, and quickly slipped a finger into me, shocking me with its effect. "Narrow and tight as ever," he said, his voice amused. He reached over and took a small object from the night table – a flexible rubber penis. I could see him flex it, and then he took a tube of lubricant from the table. He pressed its cold gel between my buttocks, and then slowly inserted the rubber penis. It felt strange but was unusually soft. It had a long leather string attached to it. "A new kind of butt plug," he said in a half mumble, and eased it into me.

Wiping the oil and lubricant off his hands, he took a little whip, leather handle and long leather strips. "Now we can begin," he said, and I tried not to tense, knowing that tense flesh feels a blow more smartly than relaxed flesh does. He felt along the band of flesh where my buttocks rose from the back of my thighs. "The ideal place to begin a good spanking," he said, and used the whip sharply, quickly, once, twice, three times. It stung, the effect lingering when he stopped. Then he used the whip again, this time higher, where my buttocks curved more roundly, two smart lashings.

"And now, to be sure the spanking is thorough." He gently withdrew the dildo and tossed it onto the bed. He bent and pulled my panties off, and pushed my knees and thighs wide apart. He took a little cat o'nine tails off the stand, and holding one cheek of my buttocks aside, he flicked the cat between my buttocks, the tender flesh stinging. Then he took a thick flat strap that was maybe a foot long, and he said, "This will make you properly red and sensitive," and he used the strap across my buttocks once. He touched them, and I could feel the soreness. He put some more oil on my buttocks and said, "One more, for good measure." And he gave me another well-placed lashing, just under the middle of my buttocks.

"Now when you sit down you will remember what happens to bad girls," he said in a mocking taunt. He wiped off the oil with a towel, which hurt as he rubbed, but he left the wet lubricant between my buttocks.

He turned me over, again making sure my thighs were wide apart, and taking the little cat, he flicked it along my crotch, then caressing the bareness, then flicking it sharply again between my open legs. He took a small vibrator and placed it over my clitoris, and took another dildo that had a vibrator and slipped it into my vagina. He watched me, amused, as he wiped his hands and unbuttoned my blouse. He could see me struggling to control my movements, pressing my lips together not to moan or cry out.

He unbuttoned my blouse and pushed it apart, open. Then he

lay across the bed from the other side, and took each breast in turn in his mouth, sucking and gently biting the nipple each time. I could not move, between the pain and the pleasure, the vibrator tormenting me, my buttocks burning, the sensation from my breasts seeming to run in a straight line downward, making me want to writhe.

He saw my reaction, and with a look of stern satisfaction, he removed the vibrators, and rolled me about to get my clothes completely off, pulling me up onto the bed so that I lay there naked. Pushing my knees apart again, he bent this time to tongue my clitoris, sucking on it and then flicking his tongue across it. I thought I would pass out with the pleasure of it.

Then in no time he was on top of me, pinning me, entering me urgently, his own moaning making me wilder, and with a half dozen thrusts he had come again, and lay there exhausted, summoning enough energy not to collapse on top of me, to let me breathe, and he rolled to the side, but still pinning half my body under his.

I was throbbing everywhere, my eyes closed, and I was about to press my thighs together when I felt his hand on my thigh. "Stay still," he ordered. Then he slowly, insistently, rubbed my clitoris, moving his fingers down to my vagina, inserting a finger quickly and then withdrawing it. He flung one leg across my thighs to hold me in place, put a small vibrating dildo in my vagina, and continued to rub my clitoris slowly with one hand, the other hand holding my hands above my head.

I wanted to mewl or moan and only barely controlled myself when he stopped and changed position, using his tongue to lick slowly the way his finger had moved over my clitoris.

"You are delicious, you bad and naughty girl," he mumbled, and wiping his wet face, he came up to face me and covered my lips in a deep kiss, moving inside me as he did so, rocking back and forth slowly so that I was in agony, and when he could not take it any longer, quick thrusts and he had come again. I was half faint from my orgasm. But he would not let up, pressing my swollen clitoris with his fingers, working me, the painful pleasure of the aftermath washing over me.

I knew he wanted to sleep. I did too. He was fighting it, not wanting to lose any time before the early summer dawn. But he could not resist, and we drifted into sleep, my last thought that it would have been so sweet without this enmity and punishment.

This time we slept barely an hour. Perhaps we were both aware that this was the final night, nervous, each of us, in different ways. He caressed my body everywhere, and put my hand on his penis, moving it so that I was pleasuring him, raising and lowering the foreskin over the shaft of him, sticky and wet, both of us. Another deep kiss and he was drawing me up from the bed, opening the door to the bathroom. This time the air and water were scented with lavender, the water warm as he led me into the tub, quickly dipping each of us, the water stinging my buttocks, then leading me out, covering me with the thick terry spa robe that also dried me off. He pulled a robe on, using it to dab himself dry, all the while leading me back into the other room.

There was a high table against one wall which I did not remember seeing last time. Rand put a stool near it, and got me up onto the table, laying me face up, the robe open around me. The table extended under my thighs, so that my knees hung off, and he pushed my thighs far apart. Pulling a padded bench from under the table he sat and pulled me toward him, entering me with his tongue, pressing inward and then withdrawing, his tongue rising each time to nibble my clitoris, a wild sensation. He could hear my ragged breath as pleasure washed over me. I opened my eyes just enough to see his satisfied look, his posses-siveness. He owned my sex, and would use me however he wanted.

He brought me down from the table, and quickly got me onto the bed, and with rapid thrusts, entered me, a few quick thrusts, and he came. I was limp.

"And now you'll see what this is for," he said, pulling me up, and moving me over to the strange half-pear that jutted up from the floor. He lowered me and turned me face downward, bending me over it, and the shape of this strange object perfectly fit me, my buttocks raised, the pillow at my head holding my forehead so that I was prone.

"Must I tie you in place?" he said, almost cheerfully, not expecting an answer. "Well, we'll have to see." He placed my hands so that each one held a post, then came behind me, and I felt the cold of lubricant being pressed between my buttocks and pressed into me, his fingers moving inside.

"How tight you are," he said, with a kind of indifferent pleasantness, a sadistic tone. I felt the soft dildo entering me, and being withdrawn, then another inserted, larger, uncomfortable, and withdrawn.

Rand was kneeling behind me now. He wiped away some of the lubricant and I felt another substance being rubbed against me. "This is supposed to relax the muscle," he said.

I bit my lip as I felt his penis pressing slowly, its tip beginning to penetrate me. He held it there, and I felt him slip a vibrator under me, against my clitoris. My buttocks were sore from his spanking, and he parted them slightly, then closed them over him as he worked the tip of his penis back and forth, starting to penetrate me, the pressure very strong, and painful as he began to press inward. I wanted to cry or scream, and I was perspiring with the effort to keep silent and bear what I knew would be even worse in a minute.

But he went no further. He simply, abruptly stopped, pulled back and stood up.

"Get up," he said, pulling me upward, though I could hardly stand. He led me back to the bed. "Lay face down," he commanded. I did, and he covered my body with his, and then he lifted me slightly, and he was inside me, but in my vagina. He pinned me as he rocked lazily and then roughly, and came with a groan. I was no more than a rag beneath him, and wondered if I'd ever move normally again.

I was so grateful to have been spared anal sex, and so wild with soreness everywhere, I was all confusion and exhaustion. I must have fallen asleep for an hour. I don't know if he slept or how long, but it was just past four in the morning, and I could hear him moving about in the sitting room. Why didn't he finish it, I wondered. Did some spark of pity finally overcome his anger at me? Whatever the reason, I was so relieved, and also hungry and dizzy, having had only juices and tea since yesterday.

The sun was starting to come up, and I was quick with washing and pulling on my own clothes from my tote bag. I did not know what to do with the Balthus outfit. My preference was to burn it, so I stuffed it into the bag. I would find an incinerator somewhere that would turn everything to ash.

As I made for the door, he was standing in the entry room, chino slacks and a shirt half buttoned, a small blue check that was the stylish casual wear for men this year. He was barefoot, and had obviously been waiting for me to emerge from the bathroom. Our bargain said silence, so I waited for him to say whatever he looked ready to say.

"I should have made our bargain include a third time," he said in a cold voice. I glanced at my phone, not trusting his clocks, careful of the terms of our bargain. It was almost six. I held the phone up and pointed at the time.

"Yes, it's over," he said. "No more silence." Then, harshly, sarcastically, he said, "I wonder what would happen if I told your brother about our bargain."

He taunted me with the casual disdain of the bully, playing on my fear of Bredon's humiliation if he found out that I had sold my body for his money. But hearing Rand make that threat, I felt my anger surge in a renewed determination to protect Bredon.

Years ago I read an interview of a Jewish man speaking of the

Holocaust, and of the relatives he tried in vain to save. Most of his family had died in the ovens, or slower deaths of starvation and abuse. His anger and bitterness were just under his words, like a creature pressing upward, trying to escape confinement. He looked self-possessed, but when he was asked to sum up his feelings, he said that if someone licked his heart, they would die of the poison. I understand that man.

Rand was watching me, anger and mockery in his face, provoking me. I just stared at him silently and coldly, but he repeated his threat.

"What if I told Bredon that you had sex with me for money, that I had taken you in every way imaginable, that I had spanked you, that I had deflowered you, that I had sodomized you?" He watched me as he spoke, looking for a reaction. I simply looked at a far wall until he was done. He had not realized how hardened I had learned to be, living with the injustice of a world that had robbed me of my parents, and almost of my sanity.

Maybe it *had* robbed me of sanity, because I felt my heart chill with calculated vengeance. If Rand thought he was taking revenge using my body, he had no idea of the fury he could unleash in me when it came to Bredon.

"If you break our bargain," I said in a pleasant voice that startled him, "if you tell, then I will tell."

He looked at me incredulously, wanting to disbelieve me, but I set my face into a grim, deadly sweetness, and said, "I will go to your parents and tell them in detail about this bargain we made. I will tell them explicitly what happened here. I would explain how your tongue explored me, and how you had raw sex with me over and over. In this house. In that tub."

I had stunned him into silence. The ring of truth is unmistakable. His face showed a mixture of anger and uncertainty. "You wouldn't," he said, his voice knife-edged.

"Oh, indeed I would. And after your *parents*, I would go to your capital partners. I know some of them are rather conservative and puritanical. I would first tell them the details of everything we did here, and then I would go to the newspapers. And then we would see who would want to be your financial partners."

I looked straight at him now. "Maybe your new partners would be the professional woman-haters, men who think women like me should be 'put in their place,' and women who hate the thought of my being young and rich."

I recited my threats as though I were discussing the weather, and watched as his expression grew more and more alarmed and angry and disbelieving.

"And then," I said with the most wicked smile I could conjure up, "I would collateralize my own fortune and launch Bredon; he and I would be capital partners, and we would simply start again."

He had seemed to stop breathing, astonished at my words. Finally he said, "You would, wouldn't you!" It was as though I had slapped his face. I had hit on his fears, just as he had tried to play on mine. He adored his parents, and his reputation for honorable behavior was a rarity among the financial wolves that circled every opportunity for gain. He was shaking his head, his fist hitting the stonework of the fireplace behind him.

"Do you really think I would tell Bredon?" he shouted again. "Do you KNOW how much I hate what I've done? And how much I hate myself that I did it?" There were tears in his eyes. "I was going to finish this bargain with a final torment, I was going to frighten you and intimidate you. So much for *my* success." Scathing words, bitterness in his voice, despair in his eyes.

I didn't know which man to trust, the tormentor or the penitent. I decided to trust neither.

"So we've kept our bargain, and we're done," I said. Calmly. Quietly.

"Yes," came the bitter assent, "oh yes. The bargain is done." He smiled a smile as bitter as his words. "I didn't wait for last night. The full amount of money was in his account two days ago. It took that long to get everything in order."

I was so relieved my knees felt weak, but I held on. "You thought I wouldn't have come here last night if I knew the money was already there," I said, pretending indifference.

He nodded.

"You really don't know me then. I would have come here anyway. That was the bargain. I wouldn't have gone back on it."

"You say that now," he challenged, "but why should you go through with it?"

"I don't know." And I really didn't know. "Maybe for pride, to prove that I keep my word." He was right, no one could say for sure what they would have done. But I was pretty sure I would have come here anyway.

What he still didn't seem to grasp was the fact that, with all the spanking and all the frantic ways in which he thought he was using me without regard for my pleasure or feelings, I had been hot for his body, his penis thrusting, his tongue in every secret place, that sexual cloud of sensation that wiped out all other thought. Yes, I was sore, and I would have memories of tonight in my body all through the coming week at least. I regretted none of that. My regret was that I could not love him back, that we had not been able to play, to recapture the joys and the sweetness of the first day we had met.

I pulled the rain cape over me and went to open the door. He was sitting by the fireplace, his elbows on his knees, his head in his hands, not looking at me as I quietly slipped out. I knew he would pull himself together enough to open the gate, and sure enough, the latch disengaged as I approached. To my surprise, his car was waiting. Tom was talking on the phone, about to hang up, and I practically ran around the block, onto the side street, out of sight of him.

The car was parked facing north, to take me home, and I wanted no witness, even Tom, to my leaving Rand's house at that hour. I was still paranoid, wanting no one to find out what I had done. I had a little time until Tom would phone Rand to ask where I was. Rand would probably tell him to cruise the streets to look for me.

In the little time I had, I ran toward a doorman and asked, please, can you call a cab for me? I made myself look nervous and naïve, and the doorman whistled a cab as it crossed the avenue, helping me into the car to my repeated thanks.

I knew Tom would drive to my apartment, and wait there if necessary to ensure my arrival. I had no intention of being there. I phoned one of the boutique hotels where we sometimes held college parties, and booked a room. St. Mary's was right down the block, a happy irony, yet one that comforted my heart.

Paying the cabdriver in cash, giving him a huge tip that had him thanking me as many times as I had thanked the doorman, I ran out of the cab and to the desk, signing in as Mary Cole. The concierge signaled a porter to show me my room, and I gave him a large bill, closed the door and bolted it, pulled off my clothes, and fell into bed into what I had as a child jokingly called "the sleep of death" – an expression I never used again after our parents had been killed.

I got back home late Saturday night to find my message light flashing. "Pls. call when home. R."

So my eluding Tom had worried him. Good. I quickly swallowed the Plan B first pill, and stored my tote with its Balthus girl costume in the secret closet. I would have to find a way to be sure it was burned in the incinerator. Stowing my Mary Cole credit card with other account material in the locked safe drawer inside the closet, I swung the door back and it became a wall again.

I sent the text, "Home," made sure all the ringers on my phones were off, and ran a soothing oatmeal tub to soak my still-sore body. Tomorrow I would call Ren, tell him I had broken up with my boyfriend, and ask him to check me out for everything.

I said an urgent prayer, addressing of all the heavenly beings I could think of, that Ren find nothing after blood tests and smears. If my body still looked sore to him, I hoped he would assume that that was the reason for the breakup.

I was exhausted with my own web of lies and subterfuge, and after soaking in the tub and feeling soothed, I lay in bed and watched comedies on television, reading in snatches from the Saturday/Sunday Times sections that I had set on the floor next to my bed. I hoped I would have the energy to go to church tomorrow. There was much to be thankful for: the Business section had large headlines with the news of Bredon's triumph in a first-of-its-kind multi-national financial deal. I felt hot tears of relief as I read the story, then turned out the lights, and prayed that the bargain and the fearfulness of these past weeks became a soon-forgotten dream.

XV

Bredon's wedding was announced for late summer, heavy vellum and rag paper invitations with their raised black lettering:

"Mr. and Mrs. Thomas Maxwell Cleves request the honor of your presence at the wedding of their daughter, Ariana Arden Cleves, to Mr. Bredon Matthews Cooper..."

There were love stamps on the invitation and reply envelopes, a concession Mrs. Cleves had made with impatient resignation after sitting with stamp dealers to find stamps that pictured at least one of their many distinguished ancestors. There were such stamps, but of such low denominations that she would have had to put stamps across the tops of the envelopes in two rows. The dealers persuaded her to use the love stamps as the best solution. They benefitted anyway, because Mrs. Cleves ordered three special albums of all the stamps with pictures of anyone related to her in American history. Many of the stamps were costly, and the order was unusual and profitable.

Robin, Dina and I had taken a week to trek around Paris, but I had to get back to be a bridesmaid for Ree. I had thought to resist, or outright decline, but Bredon looked so happy at the thought, and Ree so gracious, there was no way out except graciousness in return. Seeing Bredon's joy, I was sincere when I thanked Ree for asking me. Still, the fittings and rehearsals and the short time of preparation would make for craziness. I told Robin and Dina to stay close and help me maintain distance and sanity. They were glad to do it, to be close to what was going to be a highlight of the season, the stir, rush, and designer luxury already causing chatter in fashion and financial circles.

Thank heaven, Ree's mother was a paragon of organization and authority, a take-charge personality, but too well-bred to grate or rasp. I actually grew fond of Mrs. Cleves, who looked like a parody of an old-fashioned opera singer, all bosom and voice, insisting on her way, not to be denied. Ree's slender figure must have come from some genetic swerve, her stocky father a match for her mother's substantial presence.

Her mother's kind but insistent arrangements were actually a relief for Ree, and for all of us. Ree was spared the endless details of planning that I also would have hated. She continued her work with a high-end publisher of fine art books and scholarly books on arcane subjects, such as the life of the Beguines in Belgium, a group of non-religious celibate women whose order endured even today. The publishing company was run by an old, wealthy family who saw these sorts of books as a family cultural mission. Ree would escape to work when her own fittings were done, her gown of course a major secret, to be revealed only when she began her bridal procession.

Her mother made sure that all the women in the bridal party had closed shoes and only moderate heels, because the wedding would take place outdoors at the Cleves estate in the Hamptons, on a beautiful rise overlooking the water. Great open-sided tents were being set up for the luncheon, their sides able to be lowered and closed, and air conditioning fed into the tents if the ocean breezes failed. Emergency tents for the whole area were at the ready if it dared to rain.

The guest list was small, maybe fifty people, only closest family and friends. Parties would be given for wider circles of friends and acquaintances when Ree and Bredon returned from their honeymoon. I thought the whole idea was wonderful.

So we were relieved from the fashion books, sketches, debates, and meetings with designers. Mrs. Cleves surveyed the bridesmaids: me, and Ree's oldest brother's daughter, Charlotte; one married sister who would be matron of honor; and Ree's best friend Suzanne, who would be maid of honor. That double "honor" was a family compromise, the one thing Ree insisted on. Mrs. Cleves chose a gown that managed to flatter all our figures, and Mr. Cleves and Bredon arranged the men's formal wear.

I did not care what I wore and went to fittings as instructed, Robin and Dina with me to tease and praise, and we roamed about the city afterward. I had only made one request of Mrs. Cleves, that the gown she chose would actually cover me, showing less skin and more silk. The almost-bare wedding fashions for women made me uncomfortable. I did not understand how bridegrooms could be in such gorgeous formal dress, all covered and manly, and the brides half naked, their gowns straight across the top of their breasts, dipping to show their backs almost to their waists. I had been so admiring of the wedding gown that Kate Middleton wore, for its lacy modesty. To my relief, Ree and her mother shared my views, which made Dina and Robin cheer when I told them.

Were we throwbacks? I didn't care. We would come to Ree's house to have lunch after the fittings, and Ree's father seemed to love our presence, a trio of chatter and youth, distracting him from the wedding frenzy. Bredon reported that when we were not around, Mr. Cleves found ways to hide out, going to his office to read the paper in peace, or taking Bredon and Ren to lunch, or finding civic obligations to fulfill. I saw Ree's character in his quiet sweetness. She was so like her father. My brother was going to have great in-laws, and my only tearfulness was in my solitary times when I thought of how my parents would have loved to see my brother married. That ache in my heart made me cry when I was alone. Three years an orphan. An eternity of loss.

The one secret note through all the summer was Rand. He had never apologized for his roughness in our bargain, but a week after our parting he had sent me a text: "Can you have lunch with me today?" Just like that, as though all had always been normal and friendly between us.

The text made me flush with remembrance, but I did not want to risk anyone noticing a familiarity between us. Not until more time had passed, and I had again set clear terms with Rand about never giving away what we had done.

I texted back, "Can't."

The next day he phoned. "We can have lunch," he said, saying nothing that would give anything away. He distrusted electronic communication as much as I did.

"Maybe after the wedding," I lied, having no intention of seeing him.

There had been so much activity after our last meeting, our Paris trek, the wedding, the stir over Bredon's success in the international deal, my relief that he was now bought out of it, as was Rand. I had had no time to sort out my feelings about Rand, or to figure out anything about the two weekends with him. I only knew I was glad I had done it, for my own ridiculous passion for his body, and for Bredon above all.

Then a note came that Marilisa delivered to me. I think she thought I had an old-fashioned secret admirer, though she neither pried nor changed expression when she gave it to me. The note said, "I will be at the wedding. One dance?"

I had forgotten that of course he would be there. Would he bring a woman with him? Earlier in the summer, when Robin had returned and said his name, I had simply shaken my head, and treasure that she was, she did not raise the subject again. But I couldn't ask her now to listen for the gossip. Whoever he brought, I determined not to care. And I would not have a date per se. My escort was the groomsman who would be my partner in the wedding procession, a handsome fellow, Ree's cousin. His name was Andrew Fortier, twenty-three, in graduate school, an economics major. I would learn more about him later, but Ree gave me a rundown and a picture, and I happily nodded at the prospect of a normal, nice, regular young man to dance with and sit with and maybe get to know better after the wedding.

There would be many family members from Ree's side, few from ours. Our great-aunt Caroline Hartfield would be there, her son Holt, and his son Charles Efram. We were great-cousins, second and third cousins, but we all just called each other "cousin." There were too few of us to worry about degrees of connection. Connection itself was all that mattered. Cousin Holt's wife and daughter would be in Europe on a long-planned trip that Mrs. Cleves urged them not to cancel, reassuring them that the post-honeymoon parties would be plenty of time for all the family members to be together.

In the midst of the preparations, we took the time to attend a party for Robin's cousin, Stuart van Dehn, who had just landed a job with a hedge fund, a short path to wealth. The party was at the private club used by old money and some new money, for social functions. Stuart's father had a membership, and therefore the right to reserve the club's "events room." When the room was set up for a young people's party such as we were having, the effect would be a nightclub atmosphere, and it had a flashing retro neon sign that said "Escapes." Robin and I thought it was a perfectly good name to describe the bankers and hedge fund managers who had escaped prison and fines in the great crash some years before.

Robin had shyly invited Bredon and Ree, to thank them for being so open to our college girl trio during the wedding preparations. They had been charmed but had gently declined, telling Robin that "the young people should celebrate." As though they were so ancient, though I must confess, I sometimes felt so old compared to my age peers, my life filled with too many powerful events compressed into three short years.

I determined to be the young person that I was, though, and with Robin's encouragement to find some nice young guys for the party, I invited my cousin Charles, along with Andrew Fortier, my groomsman partner. There must have been thirty of us at the party, including Stuart's former classmates and longtime friends, and their dates and friends. Because Stuart was in his twenties, as were most of the guests, no one paid attention to the underage status of three young women. It was no problem anyway, because Dina and Robin and I had decided in advance not to drink, just in case something or someone made trouble at a time so close to Bredon's wedding. None of us was that interested in drinking anyway, Robin practically never having even wine, and Dina from a family of conservative Protestants whose old traditions held alcohol to be sinful.

We danced and joked and met everyone, but pretty much managed to hold a table for the three of us, to which Charles and Andrew also gravitated after meeting this or that person. Stuart liked Dina, it was obvious, so he spent a lot of time talking with her and dancing with her and just hanging out at our table. And my cousin Charles was the surprise for Robin.

"He's gorgeous," she whispered to me when he had gone for what must have been by now the hundredth bunch of glasses of seltzer with lime for our table. "I wish he were Jewish."

"Actually, he is," I giggled, watching her grow big-eyed. "His mother is Jewish, so he is too, right?"

"Your cousin Holt married a Jewish girl? Did they make her convert?"

"No, don't be ridiculous. This isn't the middle ages."

"Oh my God, Dray, do you know you've pulled off a miracle for me; a guy I like who's *Jewish!*"

"Think of what your mother will say," I commented drily, looking pleased with myself. She was speechless, so I said, "It's like Hanukah in Israel. '*A great miracle happened here*'."

"Ooh, you're really too much," she laughingly growled at me, but looking only at my cousin Charles.

He liked her too, and when she could maneuver to sit next to him, she told him as though casually that she was Jewish, and he said his mother was too, and he had been bar mitzvahed and also confirmed, so he was sure to find at least one way to get to heaven. Both of his ceremonies had been small events, not like the all-out blasts that Robin's two older brothers had had. Robin had declined a big party for her bat mitzvah, preferring a trip with her parents and her younger brother. On they chatted. They say that weddings are places where future spouses meet, but maybe this party would do a similar magic for Robin.

Andrew, meanwhile, was as courtly and gentle and funny as I could wish, with a sweet sense of humor, that graciousness about him that seemed to be everywhere in Ree's family. He had me laughing, which delighted him, his eyes warm and bright, very deep brown. The band had started playing a set of standards, the band leader humorously challenging the young people to do their grandparents' fox trot, so that we swarmed out onto the floor in laughing pairs.

Andrew had taken my waist very tentatively and gently as we began, but I put a firm hand on his shoulder, enjoying his youth and sweetness and the happy disbelief in his eyes that we were so easy and comfortable together. We were just close enough that I could feel his hard, strong body under the formal suit he wore, and he could surely feel enough of my curves to know that I was feeling comfortably slinky in his arms. It felt so long since I had found this much joy in the still-innocent touch of a man, it was like a sweet breeze in my soul.

"You're beautiful," he said.

"So are you," I replied, and he laughed too, and said, "I'm glad you think so!"

We danced on the crowded floor until the end of the set, maybe eight songs, each riffing into the next, then drifted back to the table. Robin had returned with Charles; Dina and Stuart were off somewhere.

I was beginning to fade beyond my happiness to keep me awake. "Andrew, I'm a truly early-to-bed type, and I have to get home. But it's been so nice, I hate to leave."

"Let me see you home," he said eagerly.

"Not necessary," I replied, reaching into the tiny pocket for my phone.

"Wow, it's a small one," he exclaimed, seeing me hit the numbers with one hand, and then the key signaling Bredon's driver.

"I hate big phones," I told him.

Robin added, "And she hates handbags and a long list of other things that most people can't do without." She said this with mock resignation, and Andrew, smiling at her, helped bring my shawl around my shoulders and led me through the crowd, attentive, happy.

As we came into the lobby on our way to my car, my happiness and sleepiness competing with each other, Andrew said, "May I call you tomorrow?"

"Oh, yes," I said. "Ree will give you my number. Tell her I said you can even text." That would be Ree's signal that it was okay to tell him.

As Andrew was handing me into the car, I saw another figure on the steps. Rand. He had a beautiful woman with him, willowy figure, both of them in formal attire. Andrew closed the door and stepped back, and I waved to him, but in a quick glance I saw Rand, turning abruptly toward me as he recognized me, his face darkly serious, angry, startling the woman beside him who evidently had been talking to him.

I pretended to see none of it, and simply smiled through the car window at Andrew, who stood at the curb as we drove away. But my heart had started pounding at the sight of Rand.

XVI

The weather for the wedding was glorious, the guests in formal morning attire, white silken banners flying from the tents, smaller banners with the gray-rose and deeper rose accents that were the bridal party colors. A kind of open altar had been set up, the sea a vast expanse beyond the rise of the estate gardens. White veiling flowed over the altar, held to posts by flowers dyed to match the bridal colors, greenery winding downward to anchor the gossamer fabric to the posts. A harpist, a cellist, and two violins, formed a kind of choir at one side of the altar, and the singer was a young woman with a compelling, beautiful voice, another of Ree's nieces, training at Juilliard. She was singing a Handel aria, the strings in perfect accompaniment. The aisle had been created wide enough for groomsmen to walk down the aisle in pairs and arrange themselves to one side of Bredon and Ren as they stood waiting for the ceremony to begin.

The music started, and the wedding supervisor, who had worked with Mrs. Cleves from the start, and who seemed to become her shadow, orchestrated the procession as we emerged from the garden room of the Cleves mansion. First, the children: one of the youngest nieces held the small basket of rose petals to strew, and her older brother held the great silk cushion with the rings.

I was next, and behind me, Ree's niece Charlotte Cleves. We wore light rose dresses and gray sashes, followed by the matron and then maid of honor, both of them in slightly deeper rose with slightly lighter gray sashes than the bridesmaids'. Our dresses were draped, the upper parts of our dresses like flowing capes that curved back behind the dress to the waist, very romantic, very unusual. The women's murmurs had started with the flower girl, in a miniature bridesmaid dress, her brother in a miniature version of the groomsmen's formal morning dress, and when Ree appeared, the effect was perfect, so beautiful in its draping and flow, summery but modest, her father controlling his tears as he walked beside her. The bridesmaids had arranged themselves in a semi-circle on the bride's side of the altar, matching the groomsmen standing on Bredon's side, and I was swallowing hard to control my tears at the sheer joy on Bredon's face as he looked at Ree, and her shining face looking at him so lovingly.

Mine were not the only tears. I heard discreet sobbing, but dared not look lest I break down completely. I knew that Robin and Dina were watching me, ready to run up and catch me if I fainted, as they had laughingly promised they would when we had the rehearsal dinner last night. I was beyond grateful to Mrs. Cleves, who without fuss had gathered my friends into the wedding as though they were my sisters, Robin and Dina very much moved by her thoughtfulness. Now, Andrew too was watching me anxiously from the other side of the altar, and I managed a smile once I gathered myself and composed myself.

Ree's great-uncle James Harlan Cleves, a retired Episcopal bishop, was going to perform the marriage, assisted by the Rector and acolytes from the local church. The old man looked splendid in his red bishop's blouse, made in pleated silk, no doubt a special gift from Ree's mother for the occasion. He had a white ceremonial surplice and stole, lace and silk, the embroidery and fabric glinting in the light. One of the acolytes stood off to one side holding the bishop's staff, its crook facing forward, and on a small table the bishop's miter. The plain cross set up behind the altar was wood and gold, the altar table holding a Bible and The Book of Common Prayer. Once Ree and Bredon were standing in front of him, he took the book, bound in dark red leather, and opened it where the silk ribbons, red and white, marked the place.

He started with a departure from the usual wording of the service, saying, "In the presence of God, of this company, of those we love who are with us, and those we love whom we cannot see, but who are among the cloud of witnesses in heaven, we come together for this joyful, solemn purpose, the marriage of Ariana to Bredon."

Dina and Robin had crept closer to the front, as unobtrusively as they could, for they could see the tears of those who knew my family, and saw me holding myself tightly together, the tears welling in my eyes, which I refused to let fall.

In another departure, the bishop, that wonderful old man said, "Who gives this couple to be married?"

Ree's parents said, "We do," her brothers and sisters each murmured, "I do," I said, "I do," great-aunt Caroline and Holt and Charles said, "We do," from where we sat or stood.

With a satisfied nod, the old bishop whispered something to Ree and Bredon, and they turned to face each other, taking each other's hands.

"Dearly Beloved," he began the traditional words, "we are gathered here together in the sight of God and in the face of this company, to join Ariana and Bredon in holy matrimony…"

It was such a beautiful service, the rings given, the vows taken, Ree and Bredon never looking away from each other except to slip rings on each other's fingers. I could see Ren was also deeply moved, perhaps remembering his wife, whom no woman could yet replace in his heart and life.

Then came the final "I pronounce you married, wife and husband, and what God has joined together, let no man put asunder." A mixture of modern and traditional language, with his quick blessing over them, and then, "You may kiss the bride," to laughter and applause from the guests and Bredon and Ree seemed to glide away together, down the aisle, tightly holding each other's arms, the bridal party following, into the garden room for a breather before being greeted for the toast and the dancing.

Mrs. Cleves had already arranged that Dina and Robin be waiting for me in the garden room, and they each took an arm, taking turns giving me a kiss on the cheek, and telling me I looked fabulous. Andrew waited his turn to come up to claim my attention, my friends whispering, "Catch you later," and running back outside to where the guests were regrouping for the luncheon. Andrew's presence was assuring, safe, and we said little to each other but smiled a lot as the rest of the party rearranged itself, the children gathered by their parents.

A little path opened and Bredon came toward me, a great hug, wordless, and I gave way to my tears, laughing and crying at the same time, Ree coming behind him, her arm around me, giving me a kiss.

"Dray, I have to admire the way you can cry and not have your makeup run," she said drily. I laughed, for I wore very little eye makeup, a swipe of color, no mascara, lots of blush to cover my paleness, lipstick which I had to have chewed off at this point.

"Come on," Ree said to the women, and we followed her into the large powder room with its couches and vanity tables, the bathroom beyond. I re-touched my lipstick but did not add shadow or more blush. The woman who had made us up this morning had done a superb job, and my "face" was mostly intact.

"There's very little to come off," she had said as I refused one after another of her proposed colors and tintings and mascaras. Then she said, "Well, that's the advantage of being so young." She had sighed comically and said, with mock resignation, "I can't get away without makeup anymore." She went on to Charlotte, who wanted much more dramatic cosmetic work.

Charlotte did look beautiful afterward, her eyes outlined and her lashes thickened, high color on her lids. I was afraid Mrs. Cleves would want us to match cosmetically, but that blessed woman said nothing when she saw all of us, varyingly made up. I thought, there's a feminist buried in there not too far under the surface, I just know it. I felt a growing love for this woman who had shown such thoughtfulness toward me, without a single direct word to call attention to her noble goodness.

When the bridal party re-emerged from the garden room to join the guests, a small band had replaced the harpist and other classical musicians. The band leader had a pleasant, mellow speaking voice, asking the guests to welcome the newlyweds, Ree and Bredon coming outside to applause and laughter, the wedding party following.

The traditional dancing began, Ree with her father, both of them tearful, Bredon with me in lieu of dancing with our mother, and we were holding each other for dear life, fighting back our own tears. Then at the quiet instruction of the band leader, Bredon danced with Mrs. Cleves, and Ren cut in to dance with her, and I danced with Ree's father. The other members of the bridal party came to the dance floor, all the wedding guests now invited by the band leader to join us. It was a happy scene, a perfect gathering for a quiet but joyful wedding. I danced with Andrew until we were asked to the tables to begin the luncheon, Ren rising to make the champagne toast to the bride and groom.

The luncheon proceeded, the first course served. Bringing Andrew with me, I went over to the table where Dina and Robin were seated with Stuart and Charles, their "plus-one's." The band was playing so that guests could dance between courses, and we sat there joking and chatting. With a sudden change of expression, Dina and Robin were looking behind me, their faces alert. Rand was standing there.

"If I may," he smiled at Andrew, and turned to me. "May I have this dance?"

My heart had started its pounding, but I was determined to appear cool, despite the rising warmth I could feel reaching my face. Andrew had stood up to make room for me to rise and join Rand, he and the other young men looking admiringly at Rand, a man of wealth as legendary as my brother, and who was known to be my brother's partner in the latest blockbuster international deal. They quickly returned to their joking with each other.

But my girlfriends were watching me and Rand. He drew me quickly to the dance floor and drew me up to him. I felt weak, my breath growing heavy, and Rand's warmth seeming to increase as he held me. I looked at a space beyond us that held nothing but sky, tents, birds, ocean, but he was looking at me intently, his distinctive cologne and beneath it, his remembered scent.

"You look beautiful, Dray," he said so that only I could hear him. As we turned, I saw the woman he had brought with him, that same tall and willowy companion he had been with on the night of Stuart's party. One of the financial moguls was trying to get her attention, her model-like beauty drawing the eyes of men all around her. But she kept looking away from them, looking at us as we danced, though I could only glimpse her face in snatches each time we turned. Her look was curious, calculating. I wondered if she was in love with Rand. He never looked away from me.

"You said you would see me after the wedding," he said in that same low voice.

"School is starting soon," I said, trying to find some excuse, but wanting to say yes. The familiar heat and throb had me concentrating on looking cool and unconcerned. Other people were dancing, but many were watching us, including Ren. Like the woman Rand had brought, Ren seemed curious and concerned.

Rand did not answer me, but simply waited patiently as we danced, waiting for another answer. "I've volunteered to sponsor new freshmen," I said, "so I'll be busy..."

"I've looked at your school's calendar. It will be at least a week before that starts." His voice was mild with amusement and that same patience. Of course he was patient, he was holding on to me, I could not exactly break free and run away without attracting even more attention than we were receiving.

"Okay," I said, "call me tomorrow."

"Say you'll have lunch with me tomorrow."

"I don't know…" I began, and his voice glided into my words, the way we were gliding around as though we had danced together for years.

"I went to Bredon's school," he said in that quiet voice, "and Bredon was one of the sponsors of new boys. I have a picture of him and me and your parents at the opening of that year."

I almost froze, but Rand's arm held me steadily, its pressure keeping me moving. I had never seen such a picture in our family albums and on the photo disks. Had Rand constructed the picture with computer trickery?

As if reading my thoughts, he said, "Bredon had a copy of the picture, he told me, but his copy was placed in the school archives."

"So I can get a copy online," I said. I kept my voice as quiet as his, so that we could not be heard beneath the music. And Rand took care to dance us away from other couples as we spoke.

"No. They don't put those pictures online. They're concerned for privacy, and the safety of the students. Lots of issues. But I have a wonderful copy."

"I could ask Bredon."

"Yes, you could," he smiled, knowing I would not raise the matter with my brother, and not today of all days, and who knows what reason I would give him later on. Then he said, "There's another way into the park where my house is."

"You're all surprises today," I said, just as quietly. "I take it you want payment for the picture."

"It would be wonderful. But I'm only asking you over for lunch."

My throbbing, and his heat, told me he was lying. I was so filled with desire for him, it was all I could do not to say, "Oh yes, and when? And, oh, God, you feel wonderful." I was in a quandary, and stalled again.

"And where is this other entrance?" I managed to ask in an even voice.

"An alley from the back street. And only if you're accompanied by me. There are no street cameras that cover that way in. Meet me and we'll duck in together." He chuckled. "I can be waiting for you at one o'clock," and named the corner where I would find him.

The dance was coming to an end. "Please say yes." Gentle. Urgent.

"Yes."

Rand escorted me to the table, thanked me formally, exchanged some pleasantries with the men, and left to rejoin his companion. I had never asked her name.

A new dance was starting, and Andrew rose, holding out his arms, and I smiled at him, glad for a chance at normality, Robin and Dina also rising with Stuart and Charles, all of us dancing the next dance before the little dinner bell summoned the guests to be seated for the main course.

Ree and Bredon slipped out as the course ended and people rose to dance again. As the servers set arrays of bite-size desserts along the tables, the music stopped, and the band leader invited the guests to a "first stage of the dessert course," and to please go to the front path of the house where Ree and Bredon would say good-bye to everyone.

They looked so happy, and so gorgeous, Ree's suit from a Parisian atelier, and Bredon's cut by his favorite Italian designer. The limousine awaited them, the chauffer in livery. Mrs. Cleves had seen to everything so perfectly, I was filled with admiration, and then the final touch. As the bride and groom made their way down the path, Ree stopped to turn and toss her special bouquet, a manageable spray of flowers, because her bridal bouquet would never be able to be tossed anywhere, it was so large. It had been made to curve into her arms and along her side, and then became the centerpiece at the bridal table. The little bouquet she tossed held sprays of sweet pea and white roses.

Ree's best friend and maid of honor caught the bouquet, which led to laughter and applause, and then servers circulated with baskets of rose petals and hulled sunflower seed, which guests took by handfuls and tossed toward the departing couple. The wind would blow the petals away and birds would eat the seed. As usual, Mrs. Cleves had thought of everything.

More laughter, waves good-bye, I felt so moved, happy for my brother yet empty as I saw them leaving. Dina and Robin were on either side of me, their arms around me, comforting me because they could see how sad I was beneath my smiles. I was wrenched at the new departures and the stages of our lives that were beginning.

XVII

The night of the wedding, Dina and Ree were with me in my apartment, the men having been told to meet us later for clubbing and dancing after we had all changed out of our wedding clothes.

My girlfriends could hardly contain themselves until we got into my apartment. Marilisa had set up for dinner for us, snacks and sandwiches in the refrigerator, a note telling me to call down if we wanted to order dinner in. None of us wanted to eat anything beyond what was in the apartment, so I called Marilisa to tell her, and we set about changing and chattering. They had loved everything about the wedding, but what they were bubbling most about was Rand.

"Oh, my God!" Dina exclaimed, for she did not know that I already knew Rand. "He's so fascinated with you!"

Robin, that wonder of discretion, said nothing about the past. She could, however, talk freely about the wedding. "Dray, the connection between the two of you felt magnetic."

Dina was nodding vigorously at this. "Lots of people in the room noticed," she affirmed. "I saw a lot of people watching the two of you dance."

Robin's look was careful. "The woman he was with is Carlotta Venter. She's a model, and is growing more famous. I think being with Rand is a help on that score."

"Do you think they're serious?" Dina asked in innocence.

"I'll have to see what the gossip is," Robin said, pretending a laugh and indifference.

"What was it like?" Dina asked me, excited for me.

"He's a smooth dancer, for sure," I said, smiling to reassure Robin as much as to answer Dina.

"He was whispering to you," Dina said.

"He went to Bredon's school," I told her. I hesitated for a

moment and then said, "He met my parents when they came to Parents' Day. Bredon was his new boys' sponsor."

Robin could see that it was all true, but that there was so much more to it. Most loyal of friends, she managed to change the subject. "He looked great," she said of Rand, "but your brother was the handsomest man there, and Ree looked so incredibly beautiful! That gown!"

By this time we had changed and were sitting in my living room, Robin lounging on the sofa, Dina and I in overstuffed chairs with their little ottomans. We were chatting about the perfect details of the wedding when I heard the low chime of my phone.

"It may be Bredon," I told them. "Be right back."

I dashed down the side hall to my bedroom and study, and my heart stopped when I saw the call was from Ren. I felt a chill. Was Bredon safe?

"Ren," I said urgently, "what is it? Is Bredon okay?"

"Oh, Dray, I didn't mean to scare you," he said, all apology, and I almost cried with relief. "Bredon's fine as far as I know, please don't be upset."

"I'm okay," I lied, shaken by the fear I had felt, and chilled with sudden cold.

"I'm only calling because I promised Bredon I would check on you," he said gently, "and of course Bredon will be calling you himself." He hesitated. "I'm sorry I didn't get to dance with you. Rand was luckier than I was."

So that was it. "You're probably a better dancer," I flattered him, forcing my voice to hold steady.

"I doubt it. He looked very smooth. And very taken with you."

"Really?" I said brightly, feeling totally false. "I'm flattered."

"Your young fellow is obviously also very interested in you," he said.

"Andrew. Yes, we are all meeting later to go dancing some

more. As long as I can stay awake," I finished, laughing sincerely this time. Oh, my sleepyhead ways.

Ren seemed relieved. "Good," he said, "I'm glad."

"Ren, if you want to come with us, join us at The Fabulous." The club that was currently most popular with the young crowd had a name that flaunted its own popularity.

"No, I'll pass, but thanks," he said, still concerned. Of course, he knew of the waxing, and I think he had his suspicions. "Take care, Dray."

"Yes, I will, thanks for calling, Ren."

"You're welcome." And then he said, out of nowhere, "I only wish I were twenty years younger."

I was startled. Ren was my godfather; what he was hinting at was like spiritual incest, but it was intriguing.

"You're not old, Ren."

"Oh yes I am," he laughed. "Maybe in another life."

"Well, I'm overwhelmed," I said lightly, play-acting to cover the mix of my feelings. "I seem to have the attention of lots of men today."

"Always," he replied quietly. "You just don't notice." A brief moment and he said, "Good-night, Dray, have fun."

"Okay, Ren, thanks, 'bye."

I just stood in front of the phone, unable to sort out the mixture of my feelings. Unwilling to keep Dina and Robin waiting, I pushed all these thoughts aside to go back to my friends and my young life.

I was warming ever more toward Andrew. The more time we spent talking and dancing, the more I liked him, which was just the opposite of what happened so often with boys I had known. I wondered if the passion I had felt with Rand could also be found with Andrew. Only time would tell, of course. We had agreed to meet for church on Sunday at Saint Mary's, but before that, I would meet Rand and get a copy of the photograph, and try to decide what to do with the storm of feelings coming from every side. Ren, the surprise. Andrew. Rand.

Well, I would see what transpired tomorrow.

XVIII

It was quiet in the city, many people having left for the last long weekend of the summer, turning the three-day Labor Day holiday into as long a vacation as possible. The weather reports predicted a summery weekend, warm but moderate temperatures. As a result, many people had left Wednesday night, others had left on Thursday, still others had escaped by Friday, so today the city seemed empty, parking spaces available at meters and on side streets, unusual, pleasant.

I had left my apartment early, taking a circuitous route by cab and then by train, as though wandering aimlessly, timing it so that I would not have to stand in the street waiting for Rand. The last thing I wanted was to stir up more of a buzz than had already almost started, rumors from the wedding of our dance. One of the onlookers had said, with a bit of envy and a bit of admiration, "They're dancing as though they were the only people on earth."

But when Rand returned to his table and Carlotta's company, and we did not even look at each other for the rest of the wedding, and I stayed with my friends and with Andrew, joking and chatting, most of the speculation had died. I knew that Ren was not really fooled, and maybe Carlotta knew it too.

So I wanted my timing to be perfect, and I arrived to meet Rand, few cars passing, few people and only at a distance, exactly at one o'clock. He was already there, in the shadow of the building, stepping forward quickly, his arm coming around me, moving us rapidly to an all-but-unseen alley behind the building, and then down the narrow walkway, two people barely able to stand next to each other, to a high solid fence. It was electronically controlled, the way the front gate was, and Rand clicked the fence open so that the panel swung ajar just enough to let us slip in, our entry quick, and the gate closed behind us.

From the alley it had looked like a wooden gate painted black, but on this side I could see it was a steel door. Rand evidently shared Bredon's concern that there always be a back way out. I vaguely wondered if there were yet another way in and out, but that was a fleeting thought as Rand's body had pressed against me in the alley and now on the loop to the stone path. It was exciting to be near him again, and without the tension of being on public display, as we had been at the wedding.

The sitting room had a table set up at one end, food already there. Everything was fresh, as usual, the special shades arranged to let in light without heating the room. There were roses in vases on the mantel, on the side tables, on the dining table, not like the ones Rand had sent from India, but beautiful, giving a light perfume.

"Do you want to wash up before we eat?" Rand asked me, as though no time had passed, as though we had not experienced nights of wild sex and wilder orgasms.

I looked at Rand doubtfully. "Sure," I said. There was another hallway which I assumed led to the kitchen. "Is there a powder room down that hall?"

"Use the big bathroom," he said, pointing to the doorway.

I moved toward it warily, and looking in, saw only a guest bedroom, all the sex furniture gone except for the high table against the wall. My stomach was all butterflies, excited, relieved, wondering how he had managed to change this room so completely. I said nothing, but quickly made my way to the bathroom, closed the door, and leaned against it, taking deep breaths. Sexual longing for him filled me, and I splashed cold water on my face, washing my hands with the gorgeous, creamy soap, the towels so thick and soft, memories and desire floating about me.

When I came out I could see Rand waiting for me in the sitting room, and quickly went to join him. "Do you have the picture?" I asked.

"It's here." He took my hand, leading me to the dining table. The photograph had been framed with non-reflective glass and narrow silver edging. It sat on a padded envelope that would protect it until I got home. Rand held the chair for me and I sat, looking hungrily at the photograph, at my parents so young, so happy and proud of their son, Bredon at fifteen, standing in front of them, Rand beside him, only seven years old. All this, five years before I was born.

I was transfixed by the photograph, lost in it, studying my parents' images with an aching sense of love and loss. My fingertips caressed their figures through the glass of the frame. My eyes felt hot with the tears that brimmed, that I willed not to fall. Finally I came back to myself, took a deep breath, and the feeling of being overwhelmed began to ebb.

"I'm glad I could give you this," Rand said quietly, sitting beside me, putting his hand over mine.

I nodded, unable to speak, not knowing how to deal with all my confusion over Rand.

"Dray, may I kiss you?" Rand pulled me up out of my chair, taking my other hand. "I've missed you. I'm so sorry for the way things went between us."

An apology. Of a sort. At last. Turning our bargain into something vague.

"You're seeing someone," I told him. "Carlotta. She was jealous that you danced with me."

"I *was* seeing Carlotta," he said, an edge in his voice.

I ignored his tone, and anyway did not believe he was finished with her. "She's very beautiful," I said insistently, wanting him to tell the truth. "She's a model, the new super-model in fact..."

"Yes, and I was one way for her to become famous," he said, that same hard tone in his voice. "When I discovered how she stayed so thin, not just all the workouts at the gym, or living on coffee..."

"Models don't eat," I laughed, "and neither do ballerinas..."

"Whatever," Rand said dismissively. "Only, she had some extra help. When I caught her doing a line of coke, that was it."

Oh God, I thought. Rand saw how startled I was, and made a sound between laughter and sarcasm. "Coke will keep you thin, for sure," he said, his face disgusted, or maybe just disappointed and hurt.

"I'm sorry for her..." I began, but Rand waved my words away.

"It's just as well. She wanted to get very serious, and I didn't have those feelings for her." He looked at me, holding my hands more tightly. "She was right to be jealous. I want you, not her, not anyone else."

I could not bear the thought of his kisses while her face was before me in my mind. I pulled away from him slightly, and his eyes showed hurt and questioning.

"I only took her to the wedding because I wasn't involved with anyone else," he said. "She thought we would make up after the wedding, but I told her we were finished."

He took one of my hands, raised it to his lips, kissed it.

"Rand, you don't know what you've picked up from her..."

"I've had every test there is," he said. "I did that before you and I had sex. I know you were afraid of unprotected sex. I'm sorry, Dray, truly." The look in his eyes began to fade to despair.

"You could have made me pregnant," I said angrily.

"I think I hoped that would happen," he said, his voice now edged with misery. "But it didn't happen." He looked at me hopefully.

"No, it didn't." I felt my anger rising.

"Make love with me," he pleaded, drawing me to him. I felt the heat of my body rising, the impossible attraction between us as strong as ever.

His hands were stroking my body, my breasts, sending little tremors through me as only his touch could seem to do.

My knees were trembling, he was reaching under my skirt, his fingers finding me, feeling me wet. "Your fur grew back, it feels so soft," he whispered.

He was drawing me toward the bedroom, kissing my neck, planting kisses behind my neck, under my hair; he breathed in my perfumes and his tongue traced my earlobe. I was all but having an orgasm just from these kisses.

Still, I hesitated, and he reached down into the drawer on the table next to the bed. He drew out a foil packet. "Safe sex," he whispered with a laugh. I recognized the packet, not latex but the thin condom that was a fine, soft covering. Not true safe sex, but no pregnancy either.

Rand lifted my skirt, pulling down my panties, bending to lick my wetness, making me crazy with desire. He quickly tore open the packet, undid his trousers and got them off. No underwear. Just his beautiful naked penis, over which he quickly rolled the condom. It glistened, so transparent. He sank down onto the bed, his penis finding me, his hands caressing my breasts under my shirt, under my bra. He was inside me in an instant, bringing my buttocks upward, pressing against me so that each thrust hit into my clitoris, rocking me with pleasure, and in the haze of orgasm I heard him groan, felt the pressure of his coming, felt him grow smaller as he quickly withdrew from me, holding the condom in place, wiping himself down with a towel he must have had on the bed. I heard him getting up, going into the bathroom for another towel, using it to towel off my wetness, and he sank down beside me again, spent.

"Oh, I've dreamed of your body," he murmured.

I finally had the strength to get up, to straighten my clothes and make myself presentable again. Rand had gone to wash, and then came out and got his trousers on again.

"You're wonderful, Dray," he said, kissing me through my hair. "And I invited you for lunch. Are you starving?" He was in high humor now, pleased with himself, with me.

I was hungry, and we went to the dining table where deli sandwiches sat in plastic wrapping on a cooling platter, glass carafes with ice inserts holding iced tea and milk and one other liquid. "Iced coffee," Rand smiled, seeing me studying it.

I wished I could only have sex with him and not have to worry about any other part of our relationship. I felt completely amoral, and could not get myself to care.

We ate hungrily, tuna salads and greens and sherbet, delicious. The photograph had been encased in its protective envelope, slipped into my tote bag to bring home.

He chatted to me happily as we ate, telling me about the first meeting of the museum trustees, of the kinds of future exhibits that had been proposed, the logistics of setting up a big show, the difficulties involved in arranging loans and transporting works of art from other museums. He spoke as though we had not been through the cruel bargain we had made, the fears that had rocked me as much as the sexual pleasure I had derived from it. He spoke with me as though our past times together had happened to other people.

My feelings and confusion were sorting themselves out as we sat there. When we had finished, and shared a sink in the big bathroom, washing our hands and faces, Rand producing toothbrushes for us, happy, as though we were a couple who were living together, lovers who had no bitterness in their past.

"Please, Dray, I want to see you naked," he said after we were all fresh and clean. "I want to undress you," he said, his tone one of courtship, persuasion. His hand traveled lightly over my body, lingering to give a light pinch to my nipple, my arousal obvious to him as I grew warmer and felt the familiar throbbing between my legs.

I did not say anything as he pulled me back into the bedroom, pulling back the coverlet to reveal soft clean sheets and fresh pillows, beautifully white, the fragrance of lavender rising from them. He undressed me slowly, kissing my breasts after he removed my blouse and bra, kissing my breasts and nipping at my nipples as he did so, carefully setting my clothes on the small loveseat, undoing my skirt, pulling down my panties, kissing me and sucking me as he knelt before me to take them off completely, his own trousers and shirt already undone and off, and then lifting me to the high table, spreading my legs, entering me slowly, taking my breath away.

He stopped and went to get another condom, rolling it on quickly, entering me again, pressing his hand down to pleasure me as he moved inward and out again.

Stopping, he brought me down from the table, over to the bed, placing my hips on a pillow, holding my buttocks in his hands, holding me up at an angle so that his thrusting sent more intense shivers of pleasure through me. I felt his fingers exploring me, first one finger, then two, entering between my buttocks, making me gasp as he continued his rhythm, holding his fingers firmly inside me, his thrusting more rapid, and I could not see through the blur of sensation, drifting away while he came with a long moaning sound, collapsing beside me, drawing out of me, wiping himself off as he pulled the condom free.

My heartbeat finally slowed to normal, I could finally see again, and I must have dozed, because I came awake with a start, the mantel clock chiming five times.

"What a wonderful lunchtime," he said with a low laugh. He had been resting on one elbow, gazing down at me, studying me. "See me every day like this," he said, courtship and persuasion in his tone.

I pretended he was just joking, smiling, rising to get dressed. The days were already growing shorter, and I wanted to be home before dark. He saw my look, and helped me up, admiring my body, caressing me as I went to wash, leaving me to use the bathroom. I had carried my clothes in with me, and put them on, grateful for their expensive resistance to wrinkling. I went out to get my sandals, and put them on.

"Rand, are we going to go out through the alley?" I was hoping he would say yes, and was relieved when he nodded. "I'll get a cab."

"Tom can drive you home."

"No, it's better if I use a taxi," I said. I was so clear now on what I felt and what I wanted to do.

"Dray, will you be with me? Can we take up where we really started that day we met?"

"I don't know, Rand." I was lying. "You live the kind of life Bredon lives, and it's fascinating, but I want to live in my own generation."

"You don't have to live with me. Just say we can be lovers, that we can have this for each other."

But I was thinking of Andrew and Robin and Dina, of our newness to the world, our chance to live apart from the scramble and sophistication of the financial world. I wanted to live free, to trek around this city and other places in the world with my friends, and not be tied to a lover who had already lived the years I had yet to experience.

"I don't intend to go sleeping with other people," I said, laughing, meaning it. Where would I find such sex, such passion? But the cost was too high, I was not willing to trade my young years even for the lusty hours with Rand. This much I owed to my parents: to live the life they had given me, to live for them, who had been robbed of their lives, of their children's years and marriages.

"All right, Dray, think about it." He looked down for a moment and seemed to gather himself. "I don't want to scare you or overwhelm you. But I do love you."

In my way, in spite of everything, I knew exactly how he felt, but it still took my breath away to hear him say it. And it still made me angry that his love had so much cruelty and hatred in it. I shivered to think of the world I would be living in if Bredon's gamble had failed.

"Your thoughts are so far away," he said, watching me. "Promise me you'll think about it."

"All right, Rand. I will." That was no lie. How could I *not* think about these times with him, this passion and heat and desire? But I could not bring myself to kiss him, the thought of his having kissed Carlotta, the thought of that dreadful world he had seen from the margins, drugs and starvation and highly-paid modeling, youth at a premium, all appearance, no depth, no substance.

"I'll call you tomorrow," he said as we made for the back gate.

I just nodded. Tomorrow morning I would meet Andrew at church. The following week I would be at college, introducing new freshmen to the traditions of our school, and showing them the different places on the university campus.

We were back on the corner where we had met, and Rand looked after me as I walked quickly to the next corner and hailed a cab. He gave a little wave before disappearing back into the shadows, finding his way back to the alley gate.

I nodded in his direction and climbed into the cab, relieved to be going home.

XIX

When Bredon and Ree returned, the Thanksgiving holiday had given way to the preparations for Christmas. The parties they held combined holiday and wedding celebrations, but Ree was not drinking anything alcoholic, for she had returned pregnant with twins. They broke the news to me on the first night of their return, our reunion so happy and excited. The twins were a boy and a girl, and names had already been picked out for them: the girl would be Catherine Elizabeth Cooper, and the boy would be Thomas Maxwell Cooper, combining their parents' names into the new generation. Catherine and Thomas, my parents, my father and Ree's father sharing the same first name.

Bredon had re-opened our parents' house on Riverside Drive, dealing with the landmarks commission, installing a small elevator to navigate from the basement to the fourth story of the house. I was co-owner of the house, and Bredon wanted to create an apartment for me, but I signed over my part of the deed to them, as a wedding present.

Bredon, being Bredon, thereupon purchased another house on the Drive, one that had gone on sale when its owner died and the heirs had argued and sued and fought, deciding in the end to sell the house and split the proceeds. He had the deed made out in my name, and told me that he would oversee renovations after his own house was done. I was in no hurry, loving my apartment, and had no intention of living in the house. I could not persuade Bredon, however. He said the house could be rented once the renovation was done, which suited me fine.

Ree and Bredon decided to set up a foundation to help children in America and abroad. In their travels they had witnessed the difficulty for children with rare or poorly understood medical conditions, especially if their parents were poor, or their medical system corrupt. To give time to the foundation,

Bredon would hire staff, at least two promising young people, to run his holding corporations and research possible new ventures. Cousin Charles was a possible hire, which excited and delighted Robin. It would be interesting to see how the staffing worked out.

To my relief, Rand was not in the city very much after our Labor Day weekend sexual romp. As far as I was concerned, it was our final time together, but to keep everything very quiet, I simply contrived to be unavailable the few times Rand was in town. Robin and Dina and I had volunteered to work with Ren at his floating clinics, and my perceptive friends saw Ren's feelings for me. They determinedly worked with me as a protective shield, knowing how difficult and strange it had to be for me. They didn't know that I was willing to deal with all these strange emotions because Ren was my best refuge and excuse when Rand did get back to New York.

I was seeing Andrew as regularly as our schedules permitted, and we had all gone to Dina's parents' estate for the Thanksgiving holiday weekend. We had become a group of six, I with Andrew, Dina still with Stuart, and Robin with Charles. Dina and Stuart had become lovers, but the rest of us were only slowly getting to that point.

With the closing of the fall semester, Robin and Dina spent time with their families, but came back to New York so that the six of us could be together to celebrate the New Year. Rand had thought he would be back by then, leaving a message asking me about New Year's Eve. Before I had to think of an evasion, he sent another message that he would not be back until sometime in January. Bredon told me that the pressures on Rand from his family, and their international holdings, was even greater than it had been.

"They're going to kill him," Bredon said at one point, shaking his head.

"Why doesn't he have help, staff, assistants? Why does he

cave in to their demands?" I was curious, though I was not really sympathetic. My own feelings surprised me. Our bargain seemed to have broken the tie I had with Rand on that first day. It was so different now. All passion, no love.

"He does it because his parents make him feel guilty, because no one else in the family is as competent, lots of reasons." Bredon looked thoughtful. "And maybe he does because he loves his family, and wants to do all this for them."

My brother put his arm around me. "The things we all do for love," he said, shaking his head again.

I smiled and hugged him, saying nothing, but oh yes, I understood very well. I knew how powerful that feeling was, to protect our families. I knew very well what I had already done, what I gladly did for love.

Afternote

Although this story is set in New York City and the names of the avenues are accurate, as well as the names of the artists and writers cited by the characters, the functioning of the museum is completely fictional. There was not, to my knowledge, the kind of Balthus exhibit at the Metropolitan Museum that is described in this story. There have been shows of his work at various places, including the Met, but the show and the visit to the museum work areas as described here, only happened in this writer's imagination.

There is a wondrous church in The Times Square area called The Church of Saint Mary the Virgin. It is extremely beautiful, a true place of faith, and I hope the references to its gorgeous interior do it justice. Its rites and music are also quite beautiful, should any reader be interested in seeing and hearing them.

The Holocaust story is one that the author heard many years ago, as survivors and their relatives were interviewed for a documentary shown on public television.

BEDROOM
BOOKS

Romance, erotica, sensual or downright ballsy. When you want to escape: whether seeking a passionate fulfilment, a moment behind the bike sheds, a laugh with a chick-lit or a how-to – come into the Bedroom and take your pick. Bedroom readers are open-minded explorers knowing exactly what they like in their quest for pleasure, delight, thrills or knowledge.